All She Can Be

Rita kissed Twigg as she had never kissed another man, a kiss that made her knees weak and her head dizzy. She knew, in that endless moment, that she had found a man who could make her feel like the woman she always knew she was.

Together they knelt and fell into a soft bed of pine needles where she offered herself to him, allowing his hands to move over her body. Mindlessly, she surrendered to his touch, barely aware that he was methodically stripping away her clothing. The night air did not chill her, not in his arms.

She grew languorous under his touch as his hands possessed her breasts, the soft tenderness of her belly, and the smoothness of her inner thighs. His mouth gently opened hers, his silken-tipped tongue exploring, tasting, caressing with a fervor that sent her senses spinning.

He gentled her passions, fed her desires, brought her to the point of no return, and smiled tenderly when she sobbed with the sweetness of her passions...

By Fern Michaels
Published by The Ballantine Publishing Group:

ALL SHE CAN BE

Fern Michaels

BALLANTINE BOOKS • NEW YORK

Published by Ballantine Books
Copyright © 1983 by Fern Michaels

All rights reserved under International and Pan-American Copyright Conventions. Published in the United States by Ballantine Books, a division of Random House, Inc., New York, and simultaneously in Canada by Random House of Canada Limited, Toronto.

http://www.randomhouse.com

Library of Congress Catalog Card Number: 82-90856

ISBN 0- 345-34812-5

Manufactured in the United States of America

First Ballantine Books Edition: March 1983

20 19 18 17 16 15 14 13 12 11

Chapter One

Soft night sounds and cool, whispering breezes at last persuaded her thickly lashed eyes to close in slumber. Stars shone in the black sky, and a mellow sliver of moon watched over the earth like a lonely sentry, protecting the lovers in the magic hush of the desert darkness.

Morganna lay quietly, listening to the slow, even breathing of the dark-eyed, raven-haired man beside her. From time to time she gently touched his cool skin to reassure herself that he was real. He was hers, totally hers, for now, forever, for all eternity. Nothing save death could take him from her.

He stirred, extending a muscular arm to bring her closer. She sighed contentedly as she laid her dark head on his broad chest, feeling the thicket of fine fur soft against her cheek. Imperceptibly his arm tightened and Morganna nestled closer, whispering soft words of endearment. She felt warm lips caress her bare shoulder and then heard her husband's soft murmur

1

as he breathed her name. "Morganna ... Morganna ..."

"Hush." She placed gentle fingers upon his face, and he turned his head to press his mouth against her sweetly scented wrist. Her skin was smooth and warm, and even in sleep he was drawn to that place where her pulse drummed in a contented rhythm. "I am here, I'll always be here," she whispered. "Sleep, my love." The soft moan of her name on his lips drew her back to their lovemaking of a few hours past. . . .

It was all there. Every last word, every last emotion. A little of her life's blood, a lot of sweat, and far too many tears. Her editor would genuinely like it, her publisher would find it salable, and her agent would pretend to love it for the fat advance payment. Her readers would not be disappointed; this was what a Rita Bellamy novel was all about. Love. Passion. Romance.

"I'm the one who's disappointed," she muttered sourly. Her eyes dropped to the last typed page still in the IBM Selectric. It was good. Over the past twelve years Rita had become a best-selling author of romantic novels, progressing steadily from obscure little Gothics to historical novels of national notice. It had been said that in a Rita Bellamy novel there was a sense of soul touching. She knew her public speculated on what kind of woman their favorite novelist was, what erotic sensual delights she had tasted, what deep and meaningful relationships she enjoyed. Only Rita herself knew that her life was empty, had been empty, and that her soul had never been touched.

Rita ripped out the paper with a fierce jerk of her hand. It was all a sham, a farce, this living through her writing. Six more chapters and *Passion in Paradise* would be finished, right on schedule. Two weeks until she met her deadline. She was a pro; she would do it. She couldn't disappoint her editor, her publisher, her agent, and her readers. What did it matter if she disappointed herself?

Now that the love scene was finished, she owed herself a breath of fresh air to shake away the shadows her characters had created. When she returned she would get into the confrontation between the hero and the heroine before the "happy ever after" ending. One of these days she was going to write a book and leave the ending hanging in the air. Just like real life.

Leaning back on her hard, wooden chair, she looked around the cottage. It amazed her that she could write in such a dreary place. Without the aid of her thesaurus the only other adjective she could come up with to describe it was "dismal." Brett had taken everything, had demanded everything, at the time of the divorce. *The* divorce or *his* divorce, never *their* divorce or *her* divorce. Those were terms she had not come to grips with in the two years that had passed. Brett demanded the divorce, wanted to be free. He had found *love*, he declared, total all-consuming love. But his charged emotions didn't cloud his thinking where salvaging material assets was concerned. He traded on Rita's insecurities as a woman and the pain of her rejection, which he masterfully inflicted. Wounded, feeling a failure and guilty into the bargain, she had stood numbly by while he packed up the gleaming decorative copper, the antique wall hangings, the colonial furniture that was so homey and comfortable. He had even taken the plaid draperies and the huge oval hooked rug she had slaved over one winter while she had been trying to prove her domesticity at a time when her professional life seemed to revolve around finances and bigger and better contracts. Now everything was gone but her pottery collection. It would be a long time before she would forget the disdainful look in Brett's eyes when he passed over her treasured one-of-a-kind pieces of earthenware.

Rita rubbed her aching temples. God, why was she still feeling guilty after two long years? The dust had settled and she was on her own, making a living at something she loved. Maybe it wasn't so much guilt as the sense of failure. If she chose to see herself as the heroine in one of her books, she would have lost patience with the character before chapter three. How tragic and besieged could a character be without becoming tiresome?

She lit a cigarette, her fifteenth, or was it the sixteenth in six hours? She looked with disgust at the littered tin pie plate which served as an ashtray. Brett had taken the dishes as well as the ashtrays. It didn't matter, she told herself, for the thousandth time. The hell it didn't, she reconsidered, inhaling a lungful of smoke. She exhaled a steady stream, hating herself and her need to pacify herself with a cigarette. After two years the melancholy was wearing off, the anger setting in, and suddenly things that hadn't mattered before mattered now.

It was a two-bedroom cottage set back four hundred feet from a gigantic natural lake in the mountains of Pennsylvania. She loved it and had fought to keep it as well as her home in Ridgewood, New

Jersey. "I'll buy your share," she had said to Brett. "Mostly for myself, but for the kids too. Take what you want, but I keep the houses." Brett's lawyers had kicked up a fuss, wanting everything sold and split down the middle. But she had held out.

This was the first time she had come to the cabin since the divorce. She should do something with this place. Two years was a long time to leave it empty and now she was literally roughing it with her sleeping bag and camping utensils. Besides, she had come here to work, not to play at camping. The two sawhorses with the old door laid over them served as a desk, and her typewriter had been transported in the trunk of her Dodge station wagon.

Crushing out her cigarette, Rita poured coffee from her thermos into a heavy mug. Fortified, she stared into space and contemplated her future and her past. Why couldn't she pick up the pieces and put the divorce behind her? Other women did; why couldn't she? Lately the wall she had built around herself was beginning to crumble. She knew it was time to get on with her life. To make a stand, to make decisions. But how?

"I just don't know you any more," Brett had said, accusing her when he had demanded the divorce. That was another thing—he hadn't asked, he had demanded. He was in love. God, that had been almost funny, and it was a pity she couldn't have laughed. Instead, she had cringed, hating herself, feeling a failure, wondering where she had gone wrong. She had failed Brett. Reluctantly, she had agreed to the divorce, believing there was something definitely wrong with her, that in

5

some way she alone was responsible for Brett's sagging ego and his mid-life identity crisis. If she were a better woman, a true woman, Brett would never have sought a divorce.

Trouble had been brewing for some time. The financial rewards of her writing were a measure of her success, and she had naturally welcomed it. More than a measure of her success, her growing bank statements were a yardstick of her independence. This was something Brett couldn't deal with—or, apparently, live with. It had occurred to Rita after some revealing statements made by Brett that men equated money with power. If a woman had a dollar that wasn't given to her by her husband, she was exactly one dollar more powerful than he wished her to be. When a woman made thousands of dollars more than her husband and really had no need to ask him for anything, that made her thousands of dollars more powerful than he. Brett had been almost calm when he told her he did not need an over-the-hill forty-year-old writer of steamy sex in his life.

Her career had cost her her marriage, but she had not offered to give it up. She had paid her dues for over twenty years, and when she had finally succeeded in achieving something, becoming a person in her own right, he had no business to expect her to give it up so he could soothe his sagging ego. What about her ego? What about her wants and desires? What about her goddamned soul? Did he even know she had a soul and how it ached to be touched?

The cigarette scorched her fingers, reminding her that it was time to stub it out. Brushing her short, chestnut hair back from her forehead, Rita walked out to the back patio and surveyed her country home. It was beautiful. The Pocono mountains loomed above her, and the fragrant smell of pine and hemlock delighted her senses. She breathed deeply, savoring the pungent aroma. The acre and a half of pine-studded land and the cabin were all hers. Her name alone was on the deed. One of these days she would have to see about attaching the children's names on the crisp, legal paper. But not now. For now it was hers alone. Her eyes were dry when she looked at the brick barbecue she and Brett had built so long ago. And the clothesline with the rusty pulley. They had rigged that together, too. A small outcropping of rock covered with dwarf pines and red maples made her draw in her breath in admiration. This wasn't exactly God's country, but it was damn close.

If the weather continued as it had, she would still be able to swim in the lake. The days remained warm, the breezes soft, the water only a shade colder than "bracing." Summer was over; the neighbors had already left for home taking their children with them. The beauty and the solitude were all hers, shared only by the man who was renting the Johnson cottage at the bend of the lake. Taking her light Windbreaker, she made her way down to the edge of the lake, her sneakers scuffing at the pebbles on the walk.

If work went well today, she would go into town tomorrow and order some furniture. Rita's clear blue eyes widened at this thought. It occurred to her that this was one of the few conscious decisions she had made in the last two years that had nothing to do with her children or her work. She smiled; it was time to lay old ghosts to rest. Time to see to her own needs and comfort. Rachel, her youngest daughter, would be coming up to the cottage soon, and she wouldn't like sleeping on the floor. Not modern, liberated Rachel.

She stopped herself from lighting another cigarette as she slowly walked along the shoreline. Perhaps she should jog. Rachel was always saying it was the best thing in the world for a thick midsection. Rita pinched her own waistline. She knew Rachel looked at her with critical eyes and had intended her remarks about exercise and running for her mother. A slight woman and considered quite attractive, Rita had taken to hiding her thickening waist with overblouses and casual shirts. Exercise was just too time-consuming. One of these days she would shed those extra fifteen pounds and firm up—if and when she felt she was ready. Her thick, curly, chestnut hair was her pride and the envy of most women. Rita considered it her one redeeming feature. To hell with blow dryers and rollers. A professional haircut and a shampoo and a good shake of the head and it dried to perfection, framing her softly rounded face and accentuating her clear blue eyes.

The sun felt good. Her eyes dropped to her watch. She'd been working since seven and it was now past one. She deserved the break. Walking out onto the rickety boat pier, she inched her way past the missing planks. She wondered what Brett was doing with his new wife right now. She wasn't quite resigned to the fact that he had married a twenty-two-year-old. The lake, christened Lake Happiness, sparkled a deep, azure blue in the bright sunlight.

Sitting down on the end of the pier, she hugged her knees. See that, Rachel? Old Mom can still get her knees up to her chest. It had been a good day. She had managed to write the love scene she had been postponing. These days, she couldn't seem to find the heart for love and romance. Her own life was so barren, so indecisive and unfocused. She laughed aloud, a soft throaty sound. Perhaps she should try her hand at science fiction? Yes, it was a good day. She had made a decision to buy furniture for the cottage, and she even thought she knew what she would choose. Not colonial. She didn't want a reproduction of what the cottage had been when she shared it with Brett. No, this time it would be something lighter, yet substantial. Not wicker; that always seemed so temporary to her. Something contemporary. Hefty pillows, eclectic decorations, bright colors with tinted glass and chrome. The kind of things she couldn't become attached to—nothing resembling family heirlooms. Bright, light, and crisp. That was the way to go.

When she went back to the cottage, she would complete the chapter, make herself dinner, and start the new chapter. Yes, it was a good day. Tomorrow would be better and the day after that better still. Slowly, she was coming out of her stupor and taking a good look at the world she lived in.

Twigg Peterson shoved his papers into an untidy pile and pushed back his chair. He had worked most of the night and again this morning, and he needed a shave and a shower. Reddish-gold hair stood on end like furbishes on a Valentine card, and he ran a long, slender hand through it, absently trying to smooth it. The one thing he hadn't counted upon when he signed the lease for the cottage was loneliness. The owner had tried to tell him that summer was over and hardly a soul ever came up here during the fall and winter, but he had ignored the advice and signed the lease. There were times, like this, when he regretted his impulse to be alone, but he was sick of sand, sun, surf, and string-bikinis. By nature he was a social animal and gregarious. He missed having someone to converse with, to share a dinner with. He had taken a two-year sabbatical from the college where he was a professor of marine biology to study the relationship between killer whales and dolphins. He had spent eighteen months in the field, traveling from the blue of the Pacific to the black waters of the Indian Ocean. Now he had six months to write his reports as well as three articles he had promised to *Marine Life* and *National Geographic*. He wished he had a dog or a cat, someone. Something. Hell, at this point he'd settle for a goldfish!

Twigg Peterson had never been a creature of discipline; he preferred doing things when the urge came over him rather than waiting for someone else's schedule. Except, of course, when he was due in the classroom. Expressive green eyes and a winning smile made him a favorite with his students, and rarely did he ever have to ask for their attention. He was tall, athletic, and sapling slim. At thirty-two he felt he knew who he was and where he was going. He wore his self-confidence like a Brooks Brothers suit. One of his students, a precocious coed who had the hots for him, said he had a grin that made a girl just want to cuddle and snuggle with him. He had shied away from her after that, as well as several others whose interests were more for the instructor than the course. It wasn't that he didn't like aggressive women; he did. But "Betty Coeds" were hardly women as far as he was concerned. They were little more than girls, all giggles and Pepsodent smiles.

Twigg's eyes went to the cluttered kitchen with its seven-day supply of dirty dishes. He was going to have to do something about the mess or he wouldn't be able to eat without risking food poisoning. And, he was out of clean dishes. Baked beans out of a can only required a fork, and it was better than slugging into town and losing precious time from his writing. What he needed now was some exercise before he hit the sheets for a nap. A couple of laps along the lake would get his adrenaline flowing. Then a shower and a shave and he'd be a new man. Slipping a cassette into his Sony Walkman and adjusting the ear set, he hooked the modular miracle onto his belt buckle and left the cabin at a slow trot. He picked up speed as his feet left the rough, pebbled walkway.

Twigg was concentrating so intently on the music piping through the earphones that he didn't see Rita until he was approaching her as she sat on the far end of the pier. A human being and a woman at that! Not that Twigg wasn't aware Rita occupied the neat cottage with the long, sweeping raised decks of aged cedar that encircled the house. He had known of her existence, but whenever he had seen her she had seemed so unap-

11

proachable, so distant, that he had been reluctant to make contact.

Rita watched the jogger approach her with some nervousness. She had seen him before, jogging at an energetic pace along the lake. With unsettling recognition, she realized that she had admired his tall, whip trim body and his easy loping grace to such an extent that the hero in her book was taking on some of his attributes. Whenever she needed to describe him, she had only to think of this man who jogged outside her cottage with the sun burnishing his hair to glinting auburn. Right now, she realized this stranger was approaching her with deliberateness. No, go away, she wanted to tell him. Don't stop, don't talk to me. I want to be alone and that means no companionship, no outside interests, not even a casual acquaintance. She debated if she should get up and pretend she was just leaving or sit and wait to see what he did. She knew she would look clumsy if she tried to get to her feet, so she opted for staying where she was.

"Terwilliger Peterson, professor from Berkeley, here on a sabbatical to write a series of articles on dolphins and whales." A wry grin split his features. "Call me Twigg, everyone else does." He sat down next to Rita and held out a hand. Rita blinked as she shook it.

"I'm Rita Bellamy. I'm a . . ."—she had been about to say a housewife—"I'm a writer and I'm here to finish my latest book."

"Jesus, I'm glad to meet you. I was beginning to get cabin fever."

"I won't bother you," Rita said hastily, wishing the man would leave. He was sitting too close and he was acting as though she was his long-lost friend. She wasn't ready for friends like this one. Out of the corner of her eye she took in his appearance. He looked like he had slept in the trunk of his car and then got rained on.

"Bother me! Bother me? I'd kill for a kind word at this moment. Tell me, what are you thinking right this moment. The truth."

Rita flushed. Rachel would know what to say to this brash young man. The truth. He wanted the truth. "I was thinking you look like you slept in your trunk and then got rained on. You do look rather . . . untidy."

Twigg threw back his head and roared with laughter. Rita looked up at his long, slender throat. How wonderful his laughter sounded. She hadn't heard anyone laugh like that in years and years.

"Rita Bellamy, you are a writer, I can tell. Untidy, huh? I'm a goddamn mess. I worked all night and have had these clothes on for two days. I'm what you could call gamey right now. I promise though that the next time you see me I'll be spruced up to the nines."

Rita flushed again. "Oh, I didn't mean . . ."

Twigg's face grew serious. "Yes you did. You said what you meant. I always tell my students to say what they mean and not beat around any bushes. Makes for less misunderstanding later on." Twigg stared into her blue eyes and was startled to see the fusion of warmth and intellect which enhanced her femininity. He blinked and mentally backed off. He wanted to sit and talk to her. Talk to her for hours. Get to know her. But this wasn't the time. Instead, he got to his feet and stood looking down at her. "I'm staying in the Johnson cottage."

Rita frowned. "I know." She didn't know if he knew where she lived and didn't offer the information.

"Nice meeting you, Rita Bellamy," he said, picking his way back toward the sandy beach. Rita nodded, grateful he was leaving.

Rita sat for another fifteen minutes wondering what Camilla and the children were doing and wondering who made the top three on the *New York Times* Best Seller List. Wondering about anything and everything except her recent encounter with Twigg Peterson. She should go back and get a letter off to Charles, her youngest son. Charles still wasn't handling the divorce the way she had hoped he would. At eighteen he could certainly make his own bed, and store-bought cookies were every bit as good as her own. Why couldn't he accept that she still loved him and would always be there if he needed her? Instead, he put obstacles in her path, daring her to fight back with him. How he resented the cleaning woman who now did the cooking and the baking and the ironing. Was that all she was to Charles ... Chuck, as he now wanted to be called? Someone to clean and bake and see to his immediate needs? The typical stereotype picture-book mother? Time was what he needed. She needed time too; couldn't any of them see that? Camilla, the oldest with three children of her own, said she understood and didn't blame her mother. Blame! Rita's spine stiffened. Blame her! When it was Brett who married a girl younger than Camilla. Brett who couldn't wait for the ink on the divorce papers to dry. No matter what Camilla said, Rita knew she blamed her in a way. That she was somehow less than perfect, less than . . . those two words, "less than," haunted her twenty-four hours a day. They had all hung guilt trips on her, and she accepted them because she truly believed in some way she was *less than.* It didn't compute. Here she was, a successful author, making pots and pots of money, and she still felt *less than.*

It was Rachel who surprised her the most, Rachel who accepted the divorce with a shrug of her shoulders. Rachel who encouraged her mother to "go for it" whatever "it" happened to be. Get out, Mom, meet men, do your thing. You're your own person, you aren't an extension of Daddy.

Rita tried to check the troublesome train of thought. Why was she thinking about all of this now? Now she had to get back to work. Or maybe she should take a ride into town and order some furniture and have it delivered as soon as possible. She didn't want Ian to see her primitive living conditions.

Ian Martin considered himself the man in Rita's life. Middle-aged, attractive, he was her literary agent and business manager, deftly handling Rita's career. He doled out advice in large doses and saw himself as her protector. She had come to depend upon him and she respected him. It was nice to have a man in her life, she admitted, and though Ian hoped for a more meaningful relationship, Rita was as undecided about her feelings toward him as she was about almost all other aspects of her life. Ian was coming to the lake to pick up her completed work and take it to a skilled typist in the city. She knew she expected him to ask him to spend the night. Pushing that thought from her mind, she concentrated on making preparations for his arrival. Groceries, furnishings.

That's what she would do. Pick up some food and a couple of bottles of wine. She would make the effort for Ian. Without realizing it her eyes circled the lake and sought out the Johnson cottage. There was no sign of the tenant.

Chapter Two

RITA ENTERED HER SPARTAN COTTAGE AND FOR the first time was truly faced with the quiet and emptiness. Living like this was ridiculous. She deserved more and had certainly earned it! Why was she constantly trying to prove herself, to punish herself?

Quickly she washed her face and hands and changed to a clean blouse. Making a shopping list, gathering her credit cards and checkbook, she prepared to leave the house. There was no need to make an inventory of the refrigerator; the only thing it contained was a half dozen eggs and a can of evaporated milk for her coffee.

Willie Nelson warbled on the tape deck in the station wagon, and she hummed along with his reedy voice. It was the only cassette of his she owned, bought impulsively despite Brett's comments about country western music appealing to vacant intellects. He had always been taking jabs at her intelligence near the end of their marriage, trying to shake her belief in herself and even in those things she enjoyed. "Sing on, Willie, honey," Rita spoke to the voice coming out of the speakers. "Your secret listener is coming out of the closet. She's a little afraid of the light of day after all this time, but she's coming out anyway."

In Maxwell's Furniture Store, Rita went up and down the aisles with the amazed salesman. She had first ascertained that delivery could be made the next day. She purchased entire display rooms, everything down to the ashtrays. Tables, lamps, modular pieces, and area carpets. As she made her choices, she felt the strain lightening between her shoulders. Everything was light, contemporary, gleaming and new. Nothing even remotely resembled the formal colonial cherry and bright chintzes which had previously occupied the cottage, and Rita worried that the house might not lend itself to this sleek style. But when she thought of the smooth varnished oak floors and light sandalwood paneling and floor to ceiling windows looking out on the open air decks, she realized it was actually contemporary in spirit. Besides, she didn't want to restore the cottage to what it had once been. She didn't need reminders.

"And send me those silk palm trees over there in the corner," she said, writing out a check for the full amount of her purchases. She had just spent eleven thousand dollars without a blink. Writing out the check made her feel good. She had worked for the money, earned the right to spend it in whatever way she wanted. There was no one to ask now, no cajoling, no reasoned arguments. She wanted it and that was reason enough. She now had four and a half rooms of new furniture which would be delivered by four o'clock the next day.

Her next stop was Belk's Department Store. In the linen department she selected coarsely woven tablecloths, bright place mats and napkins, kitchen dish towels, bath towels, sheets, blankets, bedspreads. The salesgirl thought she was an hysterical housewife as she pointed and picked, but Rita smiled and whipped out her credit card. Lastly, she bought curtains for the bedroom and simple roll-up blinds for every other window in the house. They were easy to hang, needing only a few nails to secure them to the frame, and they would offer privacy in the evening. Privacy, not self-imposed exile, Rita smiled to herself.

At the grocery store the first item on the list was a kit of hair color, some body lotion, and a huge container of bubble bath. She filled two shopping carts with groceries for the freezer and empty shelves. Last on her list was a stop to the garden department and the purchase of six hanging baskets of flowers, two containing feathery ferns. One would go over her sink in the kitchen and the other next to her desk. If she had to be indoors, she could at least look at something green. She wondered if Twigg Peterson liked plants. Researching whales and dolphins, he was definitely an outdoor man. And a Ph.D. at that! She felt heat at the base of her throat and immediately switched her mind to the characters in her novel. Only thing was, the hero was beginning to look exactly like Twigg in her mind.

Driving up the scenic road leading to her cottage, Rita passed the Baker cottage and was surprised to see Connie's prized MG sitting in the drive. Connie Baker and she had been friends for what seemed a lifetime, yet somehow as often happens they only really saw each other up here at the lake. God, it was two years since she had seen her friend! So much had happened in those two years, so much to talk about.

On impulse, Rita almost swung into Connie's drive but at the last instant thought better of it. She just wasn't in the mood right now to hash and rehash the defects and failures of the divorce. Soon, she promised herself, she would call Connie.

Deep into the history of the Dutch East India Company, Rita almost decided not to answer the phone that pealed insistently. The instant she picked it up she was sorry. It was her oldest daughter, Camilla, and if there was one thing she did not need right now this minute, it was to listen to Camilla trying to coax her children into saying "hello Grandma" despite the certainty that they would cry and scream. The least Camilla could have done was to wait until the kids were quiet before she made the call instead of trying to quiet them while Rita was on hold.

"Mother, I need a favor from you," Camilla said breathlessly, a hint of emergency in her voice covering the imperceptible whine that was always present when she knew she was about to ask the impossible.

Rita clenched her teeth. "What is it, dear?"

"You sound as though you're going to refuse even before I ask," Camilla complained, immediately putting Rita on the defensive.

Rita shifted into what she called neutral and tried to concentrate on what her daughter was about to say. "I'm in the middle of a very important scene, Camilla. You know I came up here to work, and I did ask all of you children not to call unless it was an emergency."

"Yes, Mother. But this is an emergency. Tom has to go to San Francisco over the weekend, and he said I could go along if I could find a sitter for the children. I've already asked Rachel, but she said she had a big weekend planned. You always used to go with Daddy when he went away on business," she said accusingly. "No, Jody, you can't talk to Grandma right now. She's very busy talking to Mommy! Mother, Jody wants to say hello. Here, talk to him, won't you?"

For the next few minutes Rita carried on an infantile conversation with three-year-old Jody while little Audra cried in the background. *I don't need this! I really don't need this!* Rita was telling herself over and over even while she cooed and crooned to Jody. She was ashamed of herself. They were her grandchildren! She loved them! What kind of grandmother was she that she resented this intrusion? On another level of her brain, Rita was formulating excuses to decline baby-sitting. Camilla finally returned to the phone.

"What do you say, Mother? I really need a break from these darling demons. San Francisco would be such fun at this time of the year, and Tom and I need some time together." The tone of Camilla's voice was conclusive, as though Rita had already agreed.

"Darling, it isn't as though I haven't baby-sat for you in the past. You know I love the children. . . ."

"Good! Tom and I plan to take the six-thirty out of Kennedy tomorrow evening. I'm so excited! I haven't been to California in over a year, and it was no easy trick getting my reservations at the eleventh hour."

Camilla had booked even before asking Rita. This chafed. There was starch in Rita's voice when she replied. "I'm very sorry, dear, but this weekend is definitely out. I must finish to meet my deadline. I've never been late and I don't intend to start being unreliable at this stage. Why can't you hire a baby-sitter?"

"Motherrr!" Camilla's tone was aghast. "Tom won't allow just anyone to take care of the children! You know how he is about that! You just don't know how important this is to me! There is more to life than laundry and children, you know. I remember how you used to go off with Daddy . . ."

"Yes, Camilla, I did go off with your father many times. But it was never at the last minute, and I always made preparations ahead of time. You are being unfair, dear. I don't like to refuse you, but I do have to finish this book . . ."

"Where would you have been if *your* mother put a career ahead of you?" Camilla accused. "Grandma would always drop everything to come and stay with us and you know it."

"Camilla, my mother was a wonderful help to me and she loved her grandchildren. But that hardly applies here. Grandma was alone in the world without ties or a job and she looked for ways to make herself useful. Darling, it isn't as though I haven't helped you in the past. Only last month . . ."

"That was last month." Camilla's voice was cold. "I need you *this* weekend."

"I'm sorry, Camilla, I just can't see my way clear this weekend."

"Mother, you don't even have to come back to the city. I'll drive the kids up to you. Tom and I thought we'd stay on in San Francisco for a few days. Four at the most. I need you, Mother."

Rita clenched her fist around the receiver. She almost capitulated, but something stiffened within her. "No, dear, I simply have no time for the children this weekend. If there's nothing else, I must hang up now. Say hello to Tom for me."

Rita hung up as her daughter was saying, ". . . your own grandchildren, I can't believe . . ."

When the receiver was back in the cradle, Rita sat down, nearly collapsing. Her forehead was damp with perspiration and her hands trembled. She felt guilty and angry at the same time. God, why did they do this to her? Why couldn't they leave her alone and manage for themselves? Better yet, why hadn't Camilla called upon her new stepmother for assistance, or even her father?

The clear blue eyes misted over. They think I just play at this, that I have nothing else to do. None of them had ever taken her career seriously. Wife, mother, cook, laundress, seamstress, confessor, mechanic, baker, chauffeur . . . she was never Rita Bellamy, author. Rita Bellamy, person. No, they only thought of her in direct relationship to themselves and their own needs. They looked upon her writing as a competitor, alienating her from them. Even now, when she was alone, without a husband, needing to make a living for herself, they only considered themselves.

Damn, now her mood was broken. The Dutch East India Company would have to wait. For exactly two seconds she had been proud of herself in refusing Camilla and then the guilt had set in. Undoubtedly Camilla would report to Brett that Rita had refused to care for the children. She could almost envision him shaking his head and sighing in silent condemnation.

Food. Always eat and add to the midriff bulge when you're unhappy. She could certainly do that. She had spent two hundred dollars in the supermarket and could make a gourmet meal if it pleased her. A five-thousand-calorie meal. Poking about in the fridge, she decided on sausage and peppers so that she would have something left for lunch the next day.

The headache came on with blinding force as she started to chop the onions and peppers. The sausage was simmering in a stainless steel pot along with some tangy tomato sauce. She swallowed three Tylenol and went back to the chopping board. It always happened this way. The moment the guilt set in, the headache arrived, and before she knew it she had a three-day migraine. She didn't need the migraine any more than she needed her grandchildren for the weekend. Her movements were awkward, as if being performed by a stranger as she dumped the peppers and onions into the fry pan for a few quick stirs before adding them to the sausage to simmer. She couldn't wait to get to the phone to call Camilla back. Anything to get rid of the headache, the damnable guilt. Anything.

Her trembling hand was on the receiver when she heard a voice call her name. "Rita, it's Twigg Peterson. I hate to be a bother but I let some oil bubble over and now the burners won't light. Could I impose on you long enough to fry some hamburgers. God, that smells good, what is it?"

Rita stared at the tall man through the screen door. She had to do something, say something. "Come in" was the best she could manage.

Seeing Rita's white, drawn face and the trembling of her hands, he asked, "Is anything wrong? I'm sorry if I'm intruding. I can eat them raw."

"Raw?" Rita asked, not understanding. "No, it's just that this headache came on so suddenly and it's brutal. Of course you can use the stove. What else did you ask?"

"I asked what you were cooking, it smells so good."

"Sausage and peppers. I didn't know quite what to make, so I settled for that." Damn, why did she feel the need to explain? Why was she always explaining? She'd be damned if she would apologize for the emptiness of the cabin.

"Rustic," Twigg said enigmatically. "I like sausage and peppers especially on a hard roll. Are you having hard rolls? I'll bet you are."

In spite of herself, Rita laughed.

Twigg stared at the woman and grinned. He hadn't realized how attractive she was down by the pier when she was squinting into the sun. Very expressive eyes, good features. No makeup. Natural. He bet she was a knockout when she was made-up. Late thirties, early forties, he judged. "How bad is the headache?" he asked with real concern in his voice.

Tears of frustration gathered in the blue eyes. It had been so long since anyone asked how she felt, or showed concern at what she was feeling. A stranger out of nowhere suddenly appears and I fall apart at the seams, she thought. "It's a bad one. Usually leads to a migraine and I can't afford a three-day lapse."

"Then allow me." Before she knew what was happening, Twigg was behind her, massaging her neck and shoulder muscles. She winced and closed her eyes. He had strong hands, capable hands. Was it her imagination or was the pain lessening? "Okay, now hold still and then relax. I'm going to snap your neck. On the count of three." Rita did as she was told. She heard her neck snap, crack, and then the gentle pressure was back. "There, that should do it."

The blue eyes were confused when she stared up at Twigg. "It really works. Can you guarantee it won't come back?"

"Absolutely."

"You just saved me from making a phone call that I would regret. Thank you. You wanted to use the stove, you said." He was unnerving her with his close scrutiny.

"Right. That's what I said." He held out a plate with a brown glob on it.

"What is it?" Rita asked as she stared down at what looked like a cross between hamburger and dog food.

"Actually, it's chopped meat that I think has seen better days. I should probably throw it out."

"That would be my advice." Rita smiled. The headache was gone. Thank God she hadn't called Camilla. "How would you like some of my sausage and peppers? It'll be done in a few minutes. We'll have to eat outside on the picnic table though."

"Lady, I thought you were never going to ask.

I'd love to eat with you, and if you have a beer to go with it, I'll be in your debt forever."

"Oh, do you like beer with your sandwiches? So do I," Rita confided. How comfortable she felt with him. There was no fear, no anxiety. It seemed like she had known him for a long time. Such gentle fingers.

Twigg watched her as she set about making the sandwiches. She was at home in a kitchen. He wondered if there was a Mr. Bellamy and what she was doing living in an empty cottage. He craned his neck to see if a wedding ring was in sight. He almost sighed with relief when he saw her bare hand. Maybe she didn't like rings. He liked the way she moved, the way she handled the kitchen equipment, the way she spooned the rich sauce over the sausage and then closed the roll tight so it wouldn't drip. He noticed that she made three sandwiches. His eyes asked the question. Rita laughed. "Two for you and one for me. You bring the beer. The glasses are in that cabinet over your head."

"Bottle is okay with me. How about you?"

"Okay with me too. Napkins are over there. Bring a handful. Now that you're dressed to the nines, I wouldn't want you to drip on your clean shirt."

"You noticed." Twigg grinned in mock pleasure.

"I noticed." And she had. She had noticed the tight fit of the worn jeans, the designer sneakers with their frayed laces. And the six freckles he had on his left hand. It was because she was a writer and observant, she told herself as she bit into the sandwich.

They ate in companionable silence. Twigg finished first and asked if he could have another beer. Rita nodded.

"Bring me one too," she called after him.

"How long are you going to be here?" Twigg asked.

"As long as it takes to finish my novel. A week, two, I'm not sure, and then I always need a week to unwind. There's no hurry for me to get back home, so I may stay a little longer. How long will you be here?"

"I rented the cottage for six months. It's going to take at least that much time to collate my notes, draft the research reports, and then write the articles."

How many times she had sat on this same bench and watched the sun set with Brett and the kids, but she never enjoyed it as much as she did this minute. "I love the sunsets here," she said quietly.

"The end of the day. Tell me, what are you writing? Or don't you talk about it. I heard writers are scary people and are afraid someone will wander off with their ideas."

Rita laughed. "I'm past that stage. I write romantic novels for women."

"Oh, you're *that* Rita Bellamy. I thought there was something familiar about your name. When I was doing my dolphin research, several of the biologists were reading your books. They said you were good."

Rita was pleased with the compliment. "I try. I write what I like to read."

Twigg's gaze was puzzled. "Do you put any of yourself into your novels?"

Rita contemplated her answer. "Not myself exactly. Perhaps my longings, my yearnings, some of my secret desires," she said honestly. Somehow, anything less than an honest reply to this strange new friend—and he was a friend, she could sense it—would have been cheating.

"I guess I understand that. How does your family feel about what you write?"

"They tolerate it." Damn, this man was making her talk, making her see and feel all the things she wanted to forget. Honesty again in her reply. "The children are more or less on their own. Charles is away this summer doing camp counseling and then he goes to Princeton in the fall. Camilla has her own family, and Rachel is living in an apartment in the city. They all have their own lives."

"What happened to Mr. Bellamy?" Twigg asked bluntly. He had to know and what better way than to ask outright. He held his breath waiting for her reply.

"Mr. Bellamy is remarried to a young lady, a very young lady, who is one year younger than my oldest daughter," Rita said in an emotionless voice.

"Is that bitterness I hear in your voice?"

"Yes, dammit, it's bitterness you hear. I haven't exactly come to terms with it, but I will. Any more questions?" she snapped irritably.

"Not on your life. Look, I'm sorry, I didn't mean to dredge up old wounds. Hell, yes I did, I wanted to know about you. Because I want to know you better. I've never been one to dance around something. I'm sorry if I upset you."

"It's all right. I shouldn't be so defensive. It's been two years now and time enough for me to adjust." The phone shrilled in the kitchen saving her from further explanations. "Excuse me," she said, getting up.

29

Twigg sat back, leaning against the rough redwood table. He tried not to listen, but Rita's intense voice carried clearly. It sounded brittle and defensive.

"Tom, how are you? You know I'm always glad to talk to you but I'm afraid you can't make me change my mind. I have commitments and I intend to honor them. . . . No, Tom. It's out of the question. . . . Of course, I love my grandchildren. Pay someone, Tom. There are all sorts of reputable agencies with people who take care of children. . . . No, Tom, bringing them here will not make me change my mind. I explained my deadline to Camilla this afternoon. . . . Of course, I realize how important your job is, I just wonder how important you think mine is. I try not to depend upon anyone to do things for me, Tom, and I think you can take that as good advice."

Rita listened to Tom's voice coming over the receiver. He had no right, no right at all. She listened for a few more minutes, but when he began calling Jody to the phone to ask Grandma to let him come for a visit, Rita became incensed. That was playing dirty. "Tom, that's not fair and I cannot understand why you and Camilla refuse to accept my answer. If it had been another time, even next weekend . . ." Damn, there she was making excuses again. What she needed was another beer and a course in assertiveness training. Why? She had absolutely no trouble dealing with those outside her family. Secretaries, publishers, editors, publicists, smart people, important people, demanding and exacting, and yet here she was practically pleading for Camilla and Tom to understand why she could not baby-sit for them and allow her care of the children to interfere with her writing.

"Tom," Rita said in a cool, controlled voice, "I would not make the drive up here if I were you. I have given you my answer and it stands. You must make other arrangements for the children this weekend. Have you tried Brett and his wife?" Lord, she was doing it again, trying to solve their problem for them.

"Yes, Rita, we did call and they both have colds. Besides, as Camilla says, you are their grandmother. And there's no one the children would rather be with than you."

"That's very sweet, Tom, however this weekend it is just impossible." She put conviction into her voice. The last thing she needed this weekend was the children. What with the delivery of furniture, Ian coming . . . no, it was just impossible.

"Rita," Tom lowered his voice to a level of confidence, "Camilla is quite upset. You know how she admires you, even tries to emulate you. You are disappointing her terribly. We don't understand what's come over you. You've never refused before."

"Then why is it so terrible of me to refuse this one time? No, Tom"— her voice hesitated; she had almost apologized again—"it's impossible this weekend. You are an intelligent man; I've every confidence you'll solve your dilemma. Give my best to Camilla and the children. Good night, Tom."

Twigg winced when he heard the receiver slam down onto the cradle. He had gotten the gist of the conversation and had intuitively surmised Rita's conflict over refusing to baby-sit. He heard the slight tremor in her tone, the apologetic manner.

When at last she had curtly ended the conversation, he found himself rooting for her, cheering her on. Atta girl, Rita! That took some doing, I can tell, but if it's what you want, then good for you!

"Don't ask me to explain that conversation to you," Rita said setting a fresh bottle of beer in front of him. Great God! Had she actually stood up to Tom and Camilla? No doubt she would be punished for it, and they would probably keep the children away until the next time they needed her. Realizing she was neglecting her guest, she smoothed the grim line from her mouth and directed her attention to Twigg. "Why don't you tell me about what you're writing? Are dolphins actually as intelligent as I've heard?"

"I spent eighteen months in Australia researching and studying the habits of whales and dolphins and it was fascinating. As a matter of fact, I only returned to the States a few weeks ago and found the Johnson cottage through a realtor. My eyes got hungry for the autumn colors. Change of seasons and all that. Who knows when I'll get another chance like this." Twigg was encouraged by the genuine interest Rita displayed, gazing at him intently with those remarkable blue eyes of hers. "There was one dolphin we called Sinbad who literally took my breath away. The species has developed a sophisticated sonar system. They can hear up to one hundred forty kilocycles; that's eight times higher than a human. They can dive to almost a thousand feet with no decompression problems and use eighty percent of their oxygen to the fullest advantage."

As he spoke, describing the seas, the animals,

and their habits, the conversation with Tom was already fading from Rita's mind.

"The females are more playful than the males, actually. Sinbad was an exception to the rule. The female is also the aggressor in courtship; the males don't mature sexually till they're almost seven years old. It takes eleven months for a calf to be born, and the mothers are very protective of their young."

"Most mothers are," Rita said quietly, thinking of her own role as a mother and the failures and successes she had achieved.

"I suppose so," Twigg answered. "Time for me to be getting back to work. I'll return the dinner invitation as soon as I wash my dishes. Thanks again, Rita."

"It's a beautiful evening. I'll walk along with you as far as the pier."

At the pier they said their good nights, and Rita watched him lope away down the sandy beach. She liked him, liked being with him. He made her feel good about herself. He hadn't asked any questions concerning the phone conversation with Tom nor had he given any indication that he had an opinion one way or the other about what she had done.

Twigg started off down the beach. He didn't want to go home but instinctively knew Rita needed some time to herself to mull over the unpleasant phone call. He didn't want to work on his articles; he wanted to be with Rita. He turned, making his way back to her. She was still standing on the edge of the pier. "I forgot something," he shouted, that lopsided grin lifting the corners of his mouth.

"What did you forget?" She was puzzled at the expression in his eyes as he drew close to her.

"This." His arms drew around her, holding her close to him. She realized how tall he was, towering over her, lifting her chin with the tips of his fingers to look down into her eyes. His lips, when they touched hers, were soft, giving as well as taking, gently persuading her to respond. His arm, cradling her against him, was firm, strong, but his fingers still touching her face were tender, trailing whispery shadows over her cheekbones. Having him kiss her seemed to be the most natural ending to an enjoyable evening. It was just that. A kiss. A tender gesture, tempting an answer but demanding none.

"Good night, pretty lady," he said huskily, his tone plucking the strings of her emotions. And then he was gone, leaving her standing alone while she watched him retrace his steps.

Rita moistened her lips that were so recently kissed. Soundly kissed, she would have written if it were a scene from one of her books. She had been licked by the flame of remembered passions, good lusty feelings she had thought were lost to her. Twigg Peterson was good for the ego. "Pretty lady" he had called her, and suddenly she did feel pretty and just a little bit more excited than she would have liked.

Back in his cottage Twigg faced the blank page in the typewriter. He had wanted to kiss her and he had. Wanted to kiss her almost from the moment he had introduced himself to her earlier that day. There was something vulnerable about Rita Bellamy and something strong too. How good she had felt in his arms, how sweetly she had returned his kiss. There was no need to sit here and ponder what she had thought of him, if he had offended her. With Rita, everything was up front. Black and white. She either liked you or she didn't. And that was good too. Emotional games were for children and more often they hurt rather than gave pleasure. The white page glared accusingly under the goosenecked lamp and he began to work.

Chapter Three

RITA LAY DEEP IN THE SLEEPING BAG, SNUGGLING for warmth. It was early, still dark outside, probably no later than five A.M. Soon the birds would begin their incessant chatter. Rita groaned aloud. She wasn't ready for this particular day. She would not think about Twigg. No, she absolutely would not think about the long and lingering kiss that had reached something so deeply buried within her that she hesitated to put a name to it. Instead, she would think of something else. Camilla popped into her thoughts. She had always felt closest to her oldest child, and she did not like the rift coming between them.

It had always been Camilla who emulated Rita. Playing house, caring for her dolls, liking tedious household chores, always being the first to help with the dishes. Now there was an unspoken hostility between them, and Rita didn't quite know how to mend the fences. What had she done besides refuse to immerse herself in Camilla's life? It would seem that the girl had everything she had always wanted: a home, a successful husband, children. What could she still possibly want from her mother?

Children. She wondered if she had made impossible demands on her own mother. If she had, she had never known it. Yet, before Rita's mother had died hadn't there been a distance between them? In the end, when she was so sick, her mother had decided to go to Chicago to stay with Rita's brother and his wife, as though she was loath to impose upon her only daughter. Mother, too, had resented Rita's writing. Going out to Ted in Chicago had been meant as a slap in the face, and Rita had felt it. Was that what Camilla was feeling? As though she'd been slapped? No, impossible. Yet, Rita's mother had resented the fact that her only daughter had drifted away into a professional world, no longer validating her own lifestyle by devoting herself to family and home. Just before she had died they had talked about it, openly, honestly. Was it possible that Camilla, who had always identified so closely with Rita, was feeling abandoned and invalidated?

Camilla, who had always sought to be like her mother, to be a wife, a mother, now felt Rita to be a different person entirely. A divorcee, living on her own, making decisions and involved in the world of books and business. She was still demanding that Rita set the example and prove out the rewards of a domestic life, still wanted her to validate the life she had chosen for herself.

Rita shrugged off the depression that was descending over her thinking about Camilla. There were still Charles and Rachel. She hadn't written that letter to Charles yet ... Chuck. She must remember. Chuck. And she must call Rachel and find out exactly when she planned to arrive so she could cook something special for her. The only time the model-thin Rachel ate decent food was when Rita cooked it for her.

Why should I care if Rachel eats or not? She's certainly old enough to take care of herself. And that was another thing. If she didn't remind Rachel and Charles about dental appointments, they would have a mouth full of decay. Not only did she have to remind them, she also had to make the appointments, often telephoning several times to fit their schedules.

Ian often offered to find her a secretary to see to the tedious arrangements of life, but Rita wouldn't hear of it. She did not want anyone to know what a slave she had become to her family. Ian only suspected half of her commitment to her grown children, and he doled out advice in choking amounts as to how she should deal with it. A widower with grown children of his own, he often pointed out how independent his offspring were. He would not accept that children always became independent of their fathers long before they were willing to separate from their mothers. It was an entirely different situation, she knew, but somehow could not convince Ian.

Dear, sweet Ian. Always looking out for her, protecting her, willing to take on the burden of any and all decisions if she so desired. Dependable Ian in his double-breasted suits and sparkling white shirts. A decent man, her mother would have called him. And good-looking in his middle years. Rita's eyes flew open. She was middle-aged. Ian was middle-aged. She knew there had been a smirk in the thought. She also knew if she encouraged him he would ask her to marry him. He wanted to take care of her as though she were a homeless waif needing his counseling, his protection from the big, bad world. Good, kind, safe Ian.

Perhaps she had needed protection in the beginning, just after the divorce when her emotions were like raw sores. But now she suspected she needed adventure. The sores had scabbed over and only a few of them were still terribly tender. She was just learning to enjoy this new freedom. She could eat when she wanted, do the dishes when and if she felt like it, go to bed, get up when she wanted, shop and buy whatever pleased her. She was beginning to learn to deal with mechanics and repair men. She had even engaged a gardener in Ridgewood so Charles would be free for tennis and all the sports he loved. She wasn't even lonely any more, except at night, and then a good book could ease even that. She was coping after two long years. *Twigg was too thin.*

Rita snuggled deeper into the sleeping bag. How warm and comfortable the thick down was. It was going to be a brisk day, she could feel it in her bones. A day for a sweat shirt and warm slacks. The weather in the Poconos was always temperamental. *His hair needed trimming.*

Her thoughts hopscotched to her ex-husband. He had always been an early riser, like herself, and had liked sex in the morning. She felt no shame when she wondered how he made love to his new wife. Probably with all the ardor he had shown on their own honeymoon twenty odd years ago. In many respects Brett had nesting instincts, something usually reserved for women. He liked a comfortable, cheery home. Good, home-cooked meals that took hours to prepare, shirts that had to be ironed, all fourteen of them, every week. He liked his slippers and pipe and his *Business Week* and *Wall Street Journal.* He liked the fireplace and his old sweater. Sometimes she wondered how he had managed to become as successful as he was. He had no imagination, no interest in anything outside his home and business. He had been a moderately good father, she supposed, going to the dancing recitals and the little league games. *For God's sake! Twigg was only thirty-two years old, ten years her junior!*

She wished she had a cigarette. She should get up and make some coffee. Decaffeinated of course. Fry some bacon and eggs. Maybe pancakes. Or French toast with cinnamon and powdered sugar. Did she buy syrup? She rolled over on her stomach and reached for a cigarette and drew the ashtray closer. She counted the cigarette butts. Twenty-two. Two more than a pack. The kids were always on her back about her smoking. Even Camilla had gotten little Jody to make comments. She was an adult, capable of reading and understanding the Surgeon General's medical warning. The bottom line was she liked to smoke and she had no intention of stopping. Certainly not for someone else. When she was out in mixed company she never lit up without asking if anyone minded. The cigarettes were her pacifier, her security blanket. If and when the day ever came when she didn't need them, it would be because she had made the decision. *The tobacco Twigg smoked was aromatic. Her cigarettes didn't seem to bother him.*

Rita slid back down in the sleeping bag just as the first early bird chirped. Was he sleeping or was he awake too? Would he amble by today or would he ignore her after last night? She *knew* he would be back, if not today then tomorrow.

She laced her hands behind her head and felt her stomach go taut. You couldn't see the excess flesh when you stretched out. A pity she couldn't remain in a supine position so that she would look trim and fit. Maybe she should diet and start some moderate form of exercise. Was middle age too late to take it off? Three healthy eight-pound deliveries had added unsightly stretch marks. She had read somewhere that one could never get rid of those unless one had cosmetic surgery. That was out; she wouldn't go under the knife for stretch marks. Or would she? She liked him. She liked his up-front attitude and the way he was in touch with his own feelings, his confidence, his gentleness. She wished she was half the person he was. She had so much to learn, so far to go till she could be like that. Each step was new, alien, and she had to think twice before she moved in any one direction.

The word "affair" bounced around in her head. She didn't like the word. "Relationship" sounded better. Brett had had an affair. She wondered if an affair ever turned into a relationship. She didn't think so. Brett wouldn't have given it time. An affair and then marriage. What was her name? Sometimes she couldn't remember. Oh yes, Melissa. The children pretended they didn't like her but they did. She could tell. Charles walked around with a smirk on his face after seeing his father and stepmother. Camilla was forever talking about Melissa's apple pies and lamb stew. Even Rachel said she had to respect Melissa and her "go-for-it" attitude. The fact that she "went" for her father didn't seem to bother Rachel at all. They all accepted Melissa and the new marriage and then took out their hostility on Rita in small, picayune ways. Hurtful ways, degrading ways. They blamed her and were still blaming her that the family wasn't intact.

She knew in her gut that they, all three of them, resented her career. Resented that she spent time on something that was not only creative but lucrative. They made cutting remarks about her television appearances and her magazine interviews.

Rita rolled over and lit another cigarette. Of course, when Camilla needed a ten-thousand-dollar loan, interest free, to build a swimming pool, Rita's money was more than welcome. And Charles had no compunction about accepting nine thousand for a new Trans Am. Rachel gladly took the "loan" for her new apartment security and three rooms of furniture. Rita didn't expect to get the money back, didn't want it. But it hurt that they hadn't asked their father, that they had assumed she would be more than glad to help out. There hadn't been one word about repayment. She would have demurred but it would have been nice to hear.

"All I wanted was a little respect, a little recognition for what I was doing. Goddamn it, why did it have to come from strangers? Why can't my own family see that I'm a person? I was a wife, a mother, and a writer. They had no right to force me to make a choice," she said bitterly to the empty room. Actually, the choice had been forced on her by Brett. *Thirty-two years young.*

Rita crawled from the sleeping bag and padded to the curtainless window. A low-lying mist crept across the ground like the swirly hem of a chiffon gown. In the lavender dawn she could see the diamond dew sparkle on the grass beneath the bedroom window. *Was he up yet?*

Rita turned the heat up and then made coffee. While it perked she showered and dressed. Another casual outfit of jeans and a navy blue sweat shirt. She stood in front of the mirror and then turned sideways. She sucked in her stomach and then released it. She winced. It had been a long time since she stared at herself so clinically. She had put on weight. Her new jeans with lycra were deceiving. As long as the zipper went up, she had ignored the pounds. She wondered how far the zipper would go if they were one hundred percent cotton. She made an ugly face at herself in the mirror. Then she laughed. "Who are you fooling, Rita Bellamy?" she asked her reflection.

"No one, not even myself," came the reply. "I'm almost to the top of the mountain now, and I don't intend to slide back. I worked too hard." Satisfied with her comment, she tugged the sweat shirt into place around her less-than-firm derrière and headed for the kitchen. She was who she was; it was as simple as that.

Two scrambled eggs, three strips of bacon, two slices of toast, three cups of coffee, and several cigarettes later, Rita felt ready to start her day at the typewriter. It was six-fifteen. She could work till the furniture people arrived and then she would take a break. Once everything was settled in, she would start dinner simmering on the stove and work for the rest of the afternoon. She allowed no time for visitors, for phone calls or meandering thoughts. She had to work, wanted to work. And there was the letter to write to Charles and the phone call she intended for Rachel. She could do both things while the delivery men carried in the furniture. Rachel was always on the run.

Before she sat down to start the day's work she walked to the door and flung it open. She made a pretense of staring down at the lake and the surrounding grove of pines. The sandy beach and pier were deserted as they should be at this hour of the morning. She let her eyes go to the bend in the lake and on to the Johnson cottage. There was no telltale stream of smoke wafting upwards. He was probably sleeping or working. She wondered if he had anything in the house for breakfast. She stood a moment longer, delaying the time she had to start to work. She didn't realize how intense her gaze was till her eyes started to water. She was forty-three years old and would be forty-four in another month.

Rita wrote industriously, lost in her work for the next four hours. The knock, when it came, startled her. "Come," she called as she finished typing a sentence.

"Your furniture, ma'am," a man called through the door.

An hour later all the furniture was in place. For an extra twenty dollars the men assembled the

45

bed and hung the ready-made drapes on the windows. Rita offered coffee and beer. The men accepted and they talked about the weather for a few minutes. When they left, Rita hastily made up the bed with the new sheets and bedspread. She stood back to admire her handiwork. Very colorful. She had chosen a king-size bed; she didn't know why. The old bed had been a double four-poster. The sheets she had picked from the linen department had brown and orange butterflies flitting here and there. Very fitting, just like me— free, free, free. The bedspread picked up the deep autumn colors and lent character to the knotty pine walls. The thirsty, designer sheet towels were hung in the bathroom adding still more of her own personal tastes, her preferences, her own identity.

The giddiness stayed with Rita till she sat down to write to her son. First she filled out a check for two hundred dollars. She knew it was too much, knew that Charles would view it as a buy-off and smirk to himself. One of these days she would grab him by the scruff of the neck and slap him silly, regardless of the fact that he was almost nineteen years old. She stared at the check for a long time. Finally, she drew a big X over it and wrote another one, this one for twenty-five dollars. He was Brett's son too; let him share the expenses.

She could have written an entire chapter in the time it took her to compose a carefully written letter to her only son. Charles picked everything apart. Once he saw the check he would pour over the letter looking for ways to "zap" her. Certainly, he would expect mention of the football game the day after Thanksgiving. How she dreaded it. Brett would be there with his new wife. It would be her first meeting with the new and second Mrs. Bellamy. Charles expected her to be there and she had promised. Still, she dreaded it. Charles would smirk; Brett would be oblivious to everything and anything except his new wife. Melissa would preen beneath his adoring gaze while she tried to look away to hide her anger and hostility.

It took seven sheets of paper before Rita was satisfied with her draft. She copied over the one-paragraph letter and signed it "Love, Mom."

Instead of feeling strange and unfamiliar among the new furnishings for the cottage, she was exhilarated. Here was the proof of her first decision in too long a time. The contemporary style had been bought on impulse, on the opposite end of the pendulum from the cozy colonial she and Brett had chosen. Or had it been Brett?

Her IBM now sat on a burled oak desk, and she sat on a chrome and beige director's-style chair which rolled easily on shiny ball casters. Table tops were bronze tinted glass, and the upholstered pieces were modular, accommodating themselves to different arrangements in the rectangular room. Beiges, browns, startling touches of turquoise and cream. The roll-up blinds were perfect, mobile contraptions to control the light and her need for privacy without yards and yards of dust-collecting fabric. Geometric area rugs brought the pieces together in groupings, and she took delight in the oak-veneered three-piece etagere for holding her books and knickknacks. Rita decided she had done the wise thing in purchasing entire rooms right off the display floor. She had no time for selective buying, and she knew that it was more than possible that faced with hundreds of little choices for the cottage she might have made none.

The second bedroom for Rachel was completed, even to the pressed silk flowers framed in brass and hanging over the low double bed. Splashes of orange and deep brown for the spread, rust and beige for the rug near the bed. She realized now that she much preferred it this way: clean, almost stark, color substituting for bulky furniture. Even the small dining table just off the kitchen, with its cane and chrome chairs, was perfect, utilitarian, and yet giving the illusion of space and sleekness because of its glass table top. Arc lamps and two or three startling oriental-flavored pieces, such as the vase holding tall pussy willow branches and the mural-sized picture to hang over the hearth, complemented the decor. Satisfied, more than satisfied, Rita took a tour of the cottage, appreciating everything she had bought and applauding her decision to at last make the cottage her own. Already her head was buzzing with items she would purchase when she next went to town. There were those long-stemmed glasses she had admired in Rose's, and the florist in town would create something wonderful for the dining table. Perhaps next spring she would look into getting new porch furniture. Something really colorful . . . that was next spring. Before long, winter would set in up here at the lake and snow would cover the ground.

Reluctantly, her mind went back to those times when she and Brett had escaped for those long, intimate weekends to the lake, leaving the children in her mother's care. Those had been wonderful times, much needed times to reacquaint them with each other. Too often the pressures of Brett's job in advertising would be overwhelming, and the routine chores of children and home would put a distance between them. Those long, lovely weekends. Brett would sleep late, and she would have breakfast ready for him when he awoke. Those were the best times, making love in the morning, going back to bed in the early evening with the gentle snow falling against the window.

Rita frowned. Perhaps she had been too quick to refuse Camilla and Tom. She remembered how important those times alone with Brett had been and how they had restored their love for one another until again the pressures would build and they would run away together like naughty school children playing hookey. Her eyes swung to the typewriter and then to the phone.

No. Not this time. And if she really took a good, honest look at it, those runaway weekends hadn't been all that terrific. Had they freed her from the humdrum chores it took to keep a home? Hadn't she just traded one kitchen for another? And before leaving, it was she who had stripped the beds, collected the towels and the laundry to take back to New Jersey. She still had the cooking, the shopping, the laundry, and the feeling that the time spent away from home was more for Brett than herself. It was because of *his* need to get away, the pressures of *his* job that had to be relieved. Her job had been the same regardless of where they went.

49

Still . . . she looked at the phone again, already mentally dialing Camilla's number. Determinedly she sat down at the IBM and began working. This was *her* time now, and she was doing what *she* wanted. Wasn't she?

Rita was so deep into her novel she failed to eat lunch and kept working straight through the afternoon. Once she got up for a bottle of diet soda and a quick trip to the bathroom. She rubbed her aching shoulders as she stared out the front door. Again she stared down at the lake and the empty pier. There was no sign of life from the Johnson cottage. She didn't really expect to see any signs at all. Last night was over and done with. It was the soft, dark night and the three beers that made Twigg take her in his arms. It didn't mean anything. It was only women who conjured up feelings and emotions when there were none. She was forty-three and should know better.

Thirty-two was so young to be a full professor. Thirty-two was young, period. Forty-three was middle age. Downhill on greased sneakers. Forty- three was the respite before the onset of menopause, a time for face lifts and night creams, a time to sit back and take stock, a time to stare at the rocking chair and realize it was the enemy. A time to cover the gray hairs, time to buy a chin strap, time to lay aside old ghosts.

She had literally been going down for the count until last evening. With a huge mouthful of air she had surfaced. It was a beautiful world out there, and she wanted to be part of it. And she would, in time. But time could be the biggest enemy of all. Time. Time. Time to call Rachel before she got back to work. She should call Ian but she had nothing to say. Let him call her.

It was late afternoon when Rita pulled the phone toward her and dialed Rachel's number. Rachel finally answered the phone. Rachel was a textile designer and worked at her apartment three days out of the week. "Mom, how's it going? Almost finished?" She sounded interested, like she really cared. Rachel understood deadlines.

"Fine, honey, almost done, another week and it will be ready. How are you?"

"Just great, Mom. I met the sweetest guy. I'm going to Miami with him this weekend. He's in advertising and already has an ulcer at twenty-nine. You'll love him."

"Does that mean I finally get to meet one of your young men?" Rita asked caustically. Rachel talked a lot but usually didn't do what she'd promised.

"Depends on how it works out. He's not Mr. Perfect. I may move in with him or vice versa to see how compatible we are. Again, I might not. I'll let you know after the weekend. Anything exciting going on up there?"

Rita listened and felt the vague stirrings of a headache. It was impossible to follow Rachel. This had to be her fifteenth or sixteenth man. "Not much going on here. Rather cool today. The chipmunks are out in full force. I ordered new furniture and it was delivered this morning. It looks nice," Rita volunteered.

"Mom, Camilla called me last night after your talk with Tom. She was simply beside herself. Mom, she repeated your conversation word-for-word."

There was a ripe giggle in Rachel's voice. She approved. "Way to go, Mom. I'm proud of you. She would have dumped those kids on you like she always does and go off and have a good time. That's why I said no. I take the pill. Camilla should take the pill. It was her choice and now that she has those nasty children, let her take care of them. Mom, I didn't know you had it in you."

"Neither did I," Rita said softly. "What's the young man's name, Rachel?"

"What young man?"

"The one you're going to Miami with."

"Oh, him. I had to think for a minute. Patrick, I think. Why, is it important?"

Rita bristled. "Of course it's important. How can you go away with a man if you don't even know his name?"

"Mom, don't spin your wheels. It's Patrick. Patrick Ryan. I'd like to talk longer, Mom, but Jake is coming over to work on a new design. We'll probably work through the night. I gotta go now. I'll see you Thursday."

"Rachel, I thought Jake moved out."

"He did, but we're still friends. This is a working arrangement. If he wants to sack out, that's okay. Not to worry, Mom. I can handle it. Give my regards to the chipmunks."

Rita stared at the receiver in her hand. If she didn't control herself, she was going to get a headache. If Rachel could handle it, then that let her off the hook. She didn't have to play mother and worry. Rachel was old enough to take care of herself. She wished she knew if her second daughter had any bouts with VD. Evidently not or she would have confided the fact to her mother. Rachel confided everything. Nothing was secret as far as she was concerned. Rachel was right; she was spinning her wheels for nothing. *Nada.* There was nothing she could do. Nothing she *wanted* to do. "Headache, go away," she muttered as she scanned the papers scattered on her desk. She wondered what the thirty-two-year-old professor would think of her children if he ever met them. Somehow she didn't think he would be impressed. She wasn't impressed either. Had she failed them in some way? Was she guilty of untold atrocities that would come out later when they all went through analysis? That was all in the future. This was now. She had to get through the *now* before she could worry about past and future. She liked curly hair, especially with red and gold mixed. Green eyes went with that particular shade of hair. Usually only women were lucky enough to be green-eyed. Twigg Peterson was probably the first and only man she had ever met who had green eyes. She tried to remember the color of Ian Martin's eyes. She could barely remember what Ian looked like, much less the color of his eyes.

Something strange was happening to her. She was thinking. She was feeling. The process was similar to a sleeping hand coming back to life. Pinpricks of awareness were making her alive again. She had to put Rachel from her mind and concentrate on work and dinner. Dinner. She might as well get it ready now so she could continue to work.

Stew. Stew would be good. The evening was going to be cool, and a good, hot meal always worked wonders. It could simmer for hours, needing no care, no basting, no checking. She refused to admit to herself that she was purposely making stew so there would be something left over to take to her new neighbor. What kind of middle-aged fool would do a thing like that? "My kind," Rita snapped to the empty kitchen. She switched the radio on and heard Willie Nelson singing the lyrics to some country western tune.

Her step was light as she moved about the kitchen to the beat of the music. The dredged beef cubes sizzled in the hot fat along with the sliced onions and celery, making a tantalizing aroma. She loved the smell of frying onions. Quickly, she rinsed off the vegetables and chopped them. She added water and waited for it to boil before she adjusted the heat and covered the pot. She glanced at her watch and then set the timer so she would remember to add the vegetables. A loaf of crusty, French bread was set on the counter to thaw, along with a stick of butter. There was nothing worse than trying to spread hard butter on hot bread. She wished she still had the microwave oven, but that was one of the first things Brett had carried out to the car the day the movers came. She could always get another one. There had been a time when she lived to eat; now she ate to live, she deceived herself. Food was almost secondary at this stage in her life. Binges didn't count. Everyone went on food binges at one time or another. Unconsciously, Rita tugged at the navy sweat shirt to make sure it rode down over her stomach and buttocks.

From time to time Rita sniffed the aromatic air

and then glanced at her watch. She really didn't expect him to stop by. He hadn't said anything about seeing her today, had he? She couldn't remember. Her raw, new emotions kept getting in the way of her remembering.

Chapter Four

It WAS TEN MINUTES AFTER SEVEN WHEN RITA'S stomach growled ominously. She turned off the typewriter and tidied her desk. Useless draft pages were shoved into one of the new desk drawers. She missed using the old door on the sawhorses. There had been miles of room for all her scattered research notes. This way she would have to hunt and fish for everything she needed.

She sat down to her solitary dinner at seven-forty. The French bread was browned perfectly. The stew was hearty and yet tangy. It was the tablespoon of horseradish that gave it a special touch. She ate ravenously, topping off the meal with two cups of black coffee. Lighting a cigarette, she decided to walk off the heavy dinner with a stroll down to the pier. She was almost afraid to open the front door, hating the thought of seeing lights in the Johnson cottage. Lights meant Twigg was there and hadn't wanted to see her. If she took the stew over as was her original intention, he might think she was ready to initiate something. Better to leave it behind and just take her walk down to the pier as planned. The Johnson cottage was dark. The only light came from a street lamp on the other side of the lake and was so faint and yellowish it was barely distinguishable. Maybe something happened to him. Perhaps she should walk around and knock on the door. That's what she should do, what she would have done a week ago. It was the mothering instinct in her. Rita caught herself up short. Twigg might be younger, but there was nothing motherly about the way she felt last night or right now for that matter. Tomorrow would be time enough to see if he was all right. A grown man of thirty-two could pick up the phone and ask for help if he needed it. She was listed in the phone book. Perhaps he went into town and hadn't gotten back. Anything was a possibility and she, for one, certainly shouldn't be worrying.

Rita walked out to the end of the pier and stood staring across the lake. She shivered in her light jacket. She suddenly felt the loneliness for the first time and wished Twigg were here if only to talk about the dolphins and killer whales. She liked the resonant timbre of his voice, the lazy confident way he moved. She liked to watch his slender hands which he waved about to express a point. How well she remembered the feel of those hands on the back of her neck and the way they stroked her cheeks. He was a gentle man, of that she was sure. He was Twigg Peterson, marine biologist. Why couldn't she say she was Rita Bellamy, writer? She sat down on the edge of the pier. I'm an ex-wife, a mother, a best-selling writer, she mused to herself. She stared across the water and it hit her like a bolt of lightning. Those are things I do, not who I am. I'm Rita Bellamy. Me, Rita, the person.

Something strange was happening to her, had been happening to her since she arrived. She was looking at things differently, feeling things.

She felt comfortable sitting here on the pier thinking about her life and where it was going. For the first time in nearly two years she felt comfortable with herself. She felt comfortable with her wants, and right now she wanted to talk to Twigg Peterson. She debated going back to the cottage for the stew and realized it was nothing more than a prop. She didn't need a prop. She didn't want a prop. She slithered sideways and got to her knees and then to her feet. There were still no lights on in the Johnson cottage.

Rita lengthened her stride and almost ran to the cottage. She rapped loudly and waited for some response. When none came, she knocked a second time, this time so loud her knuckles smarted. There was still no answer. Without hesitating, Rita opened the door and peered into the dimness. There was no sign of anyone. God, what if he was in the bedroom with a woman? She swallowed hard. There was only one way to find out. She reached for the wall switch and the living room came to life. Carefully, she tiptoed to the bedroom and inched the door open. Twigg lay sprawled across the bed fully dressed in the clothes he had been wearing the night before. Was it possible he had slept through the day? She had to know if he was all right before she left. She inched her way over the polished plank floor and dropped soundlessly to her knees. Satisfied that his breathing was deep and regular. She was getting to her feet when a long arm snaked out and reached for her. Caught off guard she floundered and then fell on top of a laughing Twigg. "I may be a heavy sleeper, but not that heavy. I was aware of you the minute you walked in the door."

"I wanted to be sure you were all right. I didn't see any lights and I thought . . ."

"That your sausage and peppers made me sick." Twigg grinned, his grip on her arm secure.

"No. I just wanted to see you and talk to you," Rita said honestly.

"Talk," Twigg said rolling over on one elbow. His grip never lessened as he brought his face within inches of her own. Rita could smell his warm, sleepy breath as he stared into her eyes. She felt an exultant thump of warm delight as she saw the glowing, ardent look in his gaze.

Rita tried to inch back a bit. "Now that I know you're all right I have to get back to work. Why don't you come over for lunch tomorrow if you're not too busy?" Rita asked impulsively as she struggled to withdraw her arm. Damn, she had forgotten how long his arms were.

"You're a damn beautiful woman, Rita Bellamy," Twigg said quietly.

Positioned half on the bed and half off, Rita felt awkward and flustered. She had always found compliments of any kind hard to handle. Certainly, no one had ever called her beautiful, not even Brett. She became more aware of her surroundings, the double maple four-poster and the man staring at her. But more than that she was aware of her thumping heart and her fast-beating pulse. She had to say something to this man who wanted more than she was prepared to give. She tried to pull away. His grip was firm.

"I want you in this bed next to me. You know that, don't you?" Twigg said quietly. "I think I want you more than I've ever wanted a woman before." Twigg was shocked at how true the words were. He did want her. He did desire her. Goddamn it, he *liked* her and that was something he couldn't say about too many women in his circle of friends.

Rita met his unflinching gaze. "You barely know me. Twigg, you're thirty-two years old. I'm forty-three years old, ten years older than you. Why, you're not that much older than my children." Had she responded correctly? She had come here to talk, maybe have him kiss her again. She had no intention of playing games or teasing. Did women still tease men, she wondered.

"Age is a number. I have a number and you have a number. So what. We're people with feelings and desires. Lady, I have very strange feelings where you're concerned and I sure as hell do desire you."

"A number. Yes, you're right. Age is a number but my children . . ." she broke off lamely.

"Your children have nothing to do with this, with you or me. This is something that is strictly between you and me. Don't clutter up the issue with children."

"I don't know if I can do that. I want to be friends with you. I do feel something for you, but I . . . this is new to me, and I just don't think I'm ready to . . . to . . ."

Twigg studied her. There was no pretense about this woman. Tricks, schemes, maneuvers, and all the deviousness that made for beguilement were not part of her. He released his hold on her arm and she jerked it to her side. "Look, Rita, I'm no skirt chaser, and I'm a far cry from being a womanizer. I met you, I like you, and this is more or less a natural progression of events. Damn it, I really am tuned into you for some reason. It hit me the minute I saw you on the pier. I'm being honest with you."

"And I'm trying to be honest with you," Rita said softly.

"Come here, I want to tell you something. Look at me," he commanded gently. "I take my relationships seriously. I want you to understand that I am not what the kids call a jock. I agree I haven't known you all that long, but I want to get to know you better. My body is telling me it wants to go to bed with you. I think your body is telling you the same thing. That's physical. We can deal with that when it's time. I promise I will not take advantage of you or try to trick you unless it's to get you to feed me. I'm a lousy cook. I can't be any more up-front than that."

There was a slight misting in Rita's blue eyes. "I think I can accept that," she said lightly. "Come on, I made some stew. I was going to bring it over with me, but I thought you might think I was using that as an excuse to see you. I realized I didn't need an excuse. I wanted to see you so I came. But, it's time to go back."

They walked arm in arm back to her cottage, laughing and kicking at stray pebbles. "How's the book coming?" Twigg questioned.

"Fine. My agent is coming up tomorrow evening to take back what I've finished. He'll be spending the night. In the spare bedroom," she said hastily. "I got some furniture today."

Twigg spun Rita around till she was within inches of him. "You don't owe me any explanations. I don't want you to sound defensive when you talk with me. Agreed?"

"Agreed," Rita said. They went inside and she turned the burner on under the stew.

Later, Rita sat across from Twigg, drinking a cup of coffee while he finished the last of the stew. "I think you're a hell of a lady, Rita Bellamy, and a good cook in the bargain. Let's take a walk around the lake so I can work off all that French bread."

The quarter-moon bathed the sandy beach in a silvery glow as Rita and Twigg strolled along, her arm linked in the crook of his arm. She felt happy, alive, but a bit apprehensive. Conversation was casual, beginning with the contrary weather of the Poconos and going on to Twigg's sleeping an entire day, to Rita's children. She started off with Camilla and eased into Charles, leaving Rachel for last. Rachel always needed so much explaining.

"Whatever Rachel is or isn't, you are not to blame. She's her own person, Rita. For some reason you seem to blame yourself and I can see the guilt all over your face. All of them are adults now, even your son," Twigg said lightly. "You have to cut the strings, Rita, and when you cut them, let them stay cut. They have lives and you have a life of your own. You must be very proud of yourself," he said, easing out of the painful subject of her children.

"I am. I think I'm what you call a late bloomer. I'm doing something I love doing and getting paid while I do it. As they say in encounter groups, I think I'm 'realizing my potential.' "

They were on the way back and nearing the path that wound beneath giant hanging hemlock trees that, if followed, would bring them up and around to the back of Rita's cottage. It was eerie in the darkness, but down the center of the path was a white flood of moonlight. Prickles of electricity raced down Rita's arms as she tightened her hold on Twigg.

His embrace was neither expected nor unexpected. It was natural. Rita felt herself melting into his embrace as though she had been doing it for hundreds of years. He felt good. He felt right. His arms tightened, bringing her closer to him. No words were spoken, none were necessary. Gently, she felt his lips in her hair, on her cheek and throat. Tenderly, his fingers lifted her chin, raising her lips to his own. He was pressing her closer to his chest, crushing her breasts against him. His body was hard, muscular. Rita's arms encircled his back. Without reason or logic she felt safe and secure in his embrace, and she faced her tumultuous emotions with directness and truth. She couldn't help it, she wanted this man.

Their eyes met in the moonlight and without a trace of embarrassment she was aware she could drown in that incredibly dark gaze and emerge again as the woman she wanted and needed to become.

Seeing her moist lips part and offer themselves to him, he lowered his mouth to hers, touching her lips, tasting their sweetness, drawing from them a kiss, gentle, yet passionate. As the kiss deepened, searing flames licked her body, the pulsating beat of her heart thundered in her ears.

When he released her, his eyes searched hers for an instant, then time became eternal for Rita. From somewhere deep within her a desire to stay forever in his arms, to feel the touch of his mouth upon hers, began to crescendo, threatening to erupt like fireworks. Thick, dark lashes closed over her blue eyes and she heard her own breath come in ragged little gasps as she boldly brought her mouth once more to his, offering herself, kissing him deeply, searchingly, searing this moment upon her memory.

She kissed him as she had never kissed another man, a kiss that made her knees weak and her head dizzy. She knew, in that endless moment, that somehow this man belonged to her in a way no other man could ever belong to her, for however brief this time together would be. She had found him, a man who could make her feel like the woman she always knew she was.

Twigg's fingers were gentle as they danced through her hair. He sensed what she was feeling. There are needs of the soul that go beyond the hungers of the body. His voice was deep, husky, little more than a whisper. "Will you come with me so that we can make this a night for all eternity?"

He waited for her answer, wanted to hear her say it, commit herself to it. Wordless agreement would not do for him, he realized, not with this woman whose skin was so soft and fragrant beneath his lips and whose eyes were lowered with shyness. "Tell me, Rita. It can be wonderful between us. I know it can and I want to show you."

He felt her indecision, was aware that a part of her had withdrawn from him. Intuitively, he knew that she had not been with another man since her divorce and that she felt his touch was strange and alien. He was tapping at the walls of her insecurity and he did not want to rush her, did not want to frighten her away, yet his own burning need for her prompted him to persuade, to insist. "Tell me, Rita," he murmured against the hollow of her throat, sending little tremors vibrating through her.

"Yes, yes," she whispered huskily. Was that voice her own? A voice deep and singing with desire, a woman's voice. "Twigg," she murmured against his lips, feeling them soft and moist on her own, "I want you to make love to me."

Twigg was excited by her admission, each sensation heightened because she wanted him to love her. He captured her mouth with his own, entering with his tongue, feeling the velvet of hers. Together they knelt and fell into a soft bed of pine needles where she offered herself to him, allowing his hands to move over her body, exciting her, matching his hunger with her own.

Mindlessly, she surrendered to his touch, barely aware that he was methodically stripping away her clothing. The chill night air did not touch her, not in his arms, with his body sheltering hers, giving her the warmth she so desperately needed. She grew languorous under his touch as his hands possessed her breasts, the soft tenderness of her belly, and the smoothness of her inner thighs. His mouth gently opened hers, his silken-tipped tongue exploring, tasting, caressing with a fervor that sent her senses spinning.

66

When his hand moved between her thighs, rising upwards, she moved against his touch and she heard the response to her passion in the catch of his breath and the deep, deep sound that came from his throat. "You're so beautiful, Rita. So beautiful. I love the way you want me to touch you." His voice was softer than a will-o'-the-wisp, and she wondered if she only imagined it.

He tore away his clothes, eager to be naked against her, wanting the warmth of her touch on his body. Rolling over onto his back, he took her with him, trailing his fingers down the length of her spine and returning over and over again to the roundness of her bottom. He invited her touch, inspired her caresses, always watching her in the dim moonlight, reveling in the heavy-lidded smoldering in her eyes. He wanted her to take pleasure in him, wanted her to find him worthy of her finely tuned passions. Did he please her, he wondered as she smoothed the flat of her palms over his chest, her fingertips gripping and pulling at the thicket of hairs. Her mouth found his nipples, licking, tasting, lowering her explorations to the tautness of his belly and the hardness of his thighs. He reveled in her touch, in the expression of her eyes as he took her face in his hands and held it for his kiss.

Putting her beneath him once again, he kissed the sweetness of her mouth, her eyes, the soft curve of her jaw. Her breasts awakened beneath his kisses; she arched beneath his touch.

She sought him with her lips, possessed him with her hands, her own passions growing as she realized the pleasure she was giving him. The hardness of his sex was somehow tender and vulnerable beneath her hand as she felt it quiver with excitement and desire ... for her. His hands never left her body, seeking, exploring, touching ... she wanted to lay back and render herself to him, yet at the same time she wanted to possess him, touch him, commit him to memory and know him as she had never known another man. Instead of being alien to her, his body was as familiar to her as her own. She felt her body sing with pleasure and she knew her display of passion was food for his.

Rita was ravaged by this hunger he created in her. She wanted him to take her and bring her release. "Take me," she breathed, feeling as though she would die if he did not, yet hating to put an end to excruciating pleasure.

He put himself between her opened thighs, his eyes devouring her as she lay waiting for him. Her soft chestnut hair reflected the silver of the moon, her skin was bathed in a sleek sheen that emphasized her womanly curves and enhanced the contact between their flesh. Sitting back on his heels, his gaze locked with hers as his hands moved over her body. Rita met his eyes, unashamedly, letting him see the hungers that dwelled there and the flutter of her lashes that mirrored the tremblings in her loins. His hands slipped to her sex and she cried out softly, arching her back to press herself closer against his gently circling fingers. "You're so beautiful here," he told her, watching her eyes close and her lips part with a little gasp.

He gentled her passions, fed her desires, brought her to the point of no return and smiled tenderly when she sobbed with the sweetness of her passions. She climaxed beneath his touch, uttering her surprise, whispering his name. His hands eased the tautness of her thighs, kneading the firmness of her haunches and smoothing over her belly.

When she thought the sensation too exquisite to be surpassed, he leaned forward, driving himself into her, filling her sheath with his pulsing masculinity. Her body strained beneath his, willing itself to partake of his pleasure, to be his pleasure. The fine hairs of his chest rubbed against her breasts. His mouth took hers, deeply, lovingly. His movements were smooth and expert as he stroked within her, demanding she match his rhythm, driving her once again to the sweetness she knew could be hers.

Her fingers raked his back, feeling the play of his muscles beneath his skin. She found the firmness of his buttocks, holding fast, driving him forward, feeling him buried deep within her. He doubled her delight and she climaxed again, and only then did he raise up, grasping her bottom in his hands and lifting it, thrusting himself into her with shorter, quicker strokes.

Her body was exquisite, her responses delicious, but it was the expression on her lovely face and the delight and pleasure he saw there that pushed him over the edge and destroyed his restraint. The total joy, the hint of disbelief in her clear blue eyes, the purity of a single tear on her smooth cheek, were his undoing. He found his relief in her, her name exploding on his lips.

They lay together, legs entwined, her head upon his shoulder as he stroked the softness of her arm and the fullness of her breasts. His lips were in her hair, soft, teasing, against her brow. "You're a beautiful lover," he breathed, tightening his embrace, delighting in the intimacy between them.

Rita was silent, enjoying this aftermath to their lovemaking. He had pulled her light jacket over her shoulder to ward off the chill, and his long, lean leg was thrown over hers. She was as snug as a bug, she smiled to herself, breathing in the scent of him and nuzzling her nose against the furring on his chest. His hand played with her hair as he told her how incredibly soft it was, almost as soft as her skin.

"It hasn't been this way for me in a very long time," she told him sincerely. For a moment he was so quiet she thought he had fallen asleep. Wasn't that what men did immediately after making love? Leaving the woman filled with emotions and thoughts and no one to share them with?

"I know it hasn't, Rita." She liked the way he used her name rather than the impersonals of "honey" or "sweetheart." "I knew we could share something wonderful."

Rita tilted her head, looking up into his face. "Was it wonderful for you, Twigg? Oh, that's silly. I sound as though I'm fishing for compliments and that's not what I mean at all."

He looked down at her, smiling. "Yes, it was wonderful for me. How could you think otherwise? Oh, I see," he said, suddenly comprehending. "I'm the one with all the experience, the free life-style, a part of the new morality. And I got all this experience while you were busy being faithful to your husband, and hence, I must have had sexual experiences more wonderful than tonight."

Silently, Rita nodded, burying her face against his chest; she could not meet his eyes. That was exactly what she had meant. It was still a marvel to her that he had wanted to make love to her at all. She had never considered herself a beauty nor particularly desirable. Oh, perhaps when she was young, but certainly not since her marriage to Brett had fallen apart. The beauty and sensuality she should have felt about herself was instead imparted to the heroines in her books.

Turning over until he was looking down into her face, Twigg gently touched her cheek with the tips of his fingers. "You are beautiful, Rita, and tonight was wonderful. So very wonderful," his mouth claimed hers, softly, tenderly. "I could make love to you again and again and again," he told her chuckling. "Only I don't know if I'll ever get these pine needles out of my behind. What say we run up to your place and try out that new bed of yours? I want to hold you in my arms all night long, Rita Bellamy. I don't want to leave you until you're sleeping, otherwise I might never have the strength to leave you at all."

Laughing, they ran up to the cottage, dropping shoes, leaving behind jackets and picking pine straw out of their hair. And Twigg was as good as his word. He made love to her again, tenderly, lovingly, making her feel beautiful, truly beautiful. And only when she slept did he leave her to her dreams of him, a soft, slow smile lifting the corners of her lips.

Chapter Five

RITA AWAKENED, STRETCHING LANGUOROUSLY beneath the butterfly sheets. Her first conscious thought was that something so good had to be right. As he had promised, Twigg hadn't left until she was asleep, nestled in the comfort of her own dreams. She lay quietly, allowing her thoughts to soar back to the night before. A warm flush worked its way up to her face. Making love in the woods in the middle of the night with a man she had known less than three days. In pine needles, no less! That was something Rachel would do!

She touched her flushed cheeks, felt how warm they were. Then she explored her nakedness beneath the sheets. Were her breasts fuller somehow? They were certainly more sensitive. She felt warm and wet between her legs. That was different too. She had just been starting to think of herself as "dried up," a term she had often heard her mother use after menopause. Menopause!

Christ, she wasn't menopausal yet! And she wasn't
on the pill! "Oh, no," she moaned, turning her
face into the pillow. What was it her mother had
said? Only the good girls get caught. The bad
ones are too smart. Another moan of horror. Rita
had always thought of herself as a good girl. No.
She wasn't going to think about it, but she wasn't
going to be a fool either. She liked making love
with Twigg, and if he'd have her again, she'd
gladly share her bed with him. She would do what
the big girls did, what Rachel had been doing
since she was seventeen years old. Birth control.
Sensible. Easy. Certainly practical.

Squeezing her eyes shut against the morning
light, she threw her arms up over her head. Practical! If she had been practical, she never would
have become Twigg's lover.

Lover! Was that what she was now? She blushed.
Imagine me, Rita Bellamy, a lover!

Her body felt a renewed bite of desire as she
remembered the night before in Twigg's arms. He
had loved her, totally, completely. Seeming to enjoy
it. No, not seeming. He had enjoyed it! She knew
from the way he touched her, kissed her, loved
her. Why should she doubt him now? Just because
he had admitted to her that he was finding staying
in the Johnson cottage intolerably lonely? There
were plenty of girls in town, and with his charm
and good looks it wouldn't be difficult to persuade
someone to share his bed. Girls. Is that how she
had thought of herself, just for an instant? The
Women's Liberation Movement would be aghast
to know that she, Rita Bellamy, nearly forty-four
years old, had thought of herself as a girl. As they
would have it, from the age of five on, the mem-

bers of the female sex were supposed to think of themselves as women.

That was just plain stupid. Of course she was a woman, but was it so wrong to admit, even for a moment, that within her nearly forty-four-year-old breast beat the heart of a sixteen-year-old girl? That she could feel a hunger for a man just by remembering the feel of his hands on her flesh and the sound of his voice in her ear as he told her how beautiful she was, how desirable he found her? No, it wasn't stupid, it was delicious, and she was going to enjoy it for all it was worth.

For the entire time she was in Twigg's arms she forgot about the age difference and the midriff bulge and the not-so-firm breasts. But now, suddenly, in the full light of day, those same fears came back to punish her. What was Twigg thinking, feeling? She wished she knew. She groaned and rolled over in the bed. How empty it was. A smile tugged at her mouth. She would take a bed of pine needles any day of the week. If he had said she was lovely, desirable, then she was. Period. And she wouldn't spoil it all by thinking she had made a fool of herself. All she wanted to think about was how his eyes had greedily devoured her and how his hands and body had reminded her she was a woman.

She moved beneath the sheets, feeling the ache and soreness in her thighs. It was a good ache, a good soreness, proof that she had not dreamed last night but had actually lived it.

Touching herself, she smoothed the flat of her hand over her belly and downward. He had said she was beautiful there. His words came back to her, his voice, the sound of his whisper, shooting new thrills and excitement through her.

He had stayed awake, caressing her, loving her, until she had been the first to fall asleep. And she had slept in the crook of his arm, feeling completely at ease as though it were the most natural thing in the world.

The ticking of the clock invaded her reverie. Glancing at the clock, she realized it was nearly nine o'clock! There was a spring in her step when she bounded out of bed and headed for the shower. That certainly was a positive. She hadn't bounded out of bed since Charles was seven years old and had croup in the middle of the night.

No breakfast this morning. Quickly, she towel-dried herself and dressed in dark slacks and a shirt of watermelon cotton. She had invited Twigg for lunch. She was behind in her work and Ian was due this evening. God, she was going to have to hustle if she was to get anything done. Tuna for lunch. If it was good enough for her, it would be good enough for Twigg. She fished around in the freezer for a package of chicken and set it to thaw on the sink. Ian liked broiled chicken in lemon and butter.

Cigarette in one hand, coffee in the other, Rita stared at the blank paper in the machine. Don't fail me now, she pleaded. Don't make me regret last night. With all her willpower she forced her mind back in time to the seventeenth century and the Dutch East India Company and the trouble she had created for her characters. Today she was going to have them set sail for Sumatra and be hijacked by marauding pirates. She had to concentrate and make sure there were no loose ends anywhere. Imagination, go to work, she ordered as she turned the machine on.

Nearly two hours later she broke for a cigarette and another cup of coffee. Work was going well. She could spare the ten minutes to shift into neutral and rub her aching shoulders. She could feel the tenseness and the expectation as the hands on her watch crawled closer to the time Twigg would arrive for lunch. One o'clock she had said. It was barely eleven now. She had plenty of time before she had to make up the tuna salad.

Lunch was enjoyable. They sat in Rita's copper and brick kitchen with the new hanging fern in complete contentment. There was none of the awkwardness that Rita had feared, no gaps in the conversation. Instead, there had been smiling eye contact, shared laughter, and hearty appetites. It was Rita who glanced at her watch and signaled that lunch was over. Twigg obliged by getting up, kissing her soundly on the mouth. "I have to know something, Rita," he said seriously. "Was there any time last night when you thought about those twelve years? The truth now."

Rita grinned. "Not one minute. If you find yourself at loose ends tonight and want to take a break, why don't you come by and meet Ian? I'm sure he'll enjoy meeting you and you'll have lots in common. Maybe he can even find a market for your articles. Don't feel you have to come; it's an invitation, pure and simple."

Twigg loped back to his cottage, his steps springy and buoyant. Damn, he felt good. Rita made him feel good. At lunch she had been so helpful when he discussed his work with her, suggesting he might approach the article from a different point of view.

Perhaps he would walk over to meet Ian Martin, if only to see what he was like. In his gut he knew the friend-agent had more than a professional interest in Rita. It was obvious the way she talked about him. Yes, he would like to meet the man. Ian Martin would have to be a blind fool not to see Rita for the woman she was: talented, interesting, beautiful.

Leaning against the porch rail, his tall, lean frame striking an angular pose, Twigg tamped and lit his pipe. She had the clearest blue eyes he had ever seen. And she loved the sea, she had told him. And talking to her, discussing things with her, was enlightening, challenging. That was one lady who had an opinion, but unlike others he had known, she was also willing to see the other side.

Drawing on the pipe, the pungent smoke filling his mouth, his thoughts went back to the night before, as they had through most of the day. Rita Bellamy, woman, writer, beautiful lover. She had a way of making a man feel cherished. He laughed. It even sounded silly to him that a man would need cherishing; that was something women said they wanted from a man. But a man needed it too, needed to feel important and worthy. He could still almost feel the tenderness of her soft arms as they surrounded him, bringing him to her, welcoming him. There was an honesty about her, sharp and clear, with none of the calculating withholding he had experienced so many times before. She was exciting and stimulating and downright sexy. And yet, she was vulnerable too, and he supposed that was what made her seem so young to him, with a special brand of innocence that was lost to most women before they hit twenty.

Twigg frowned. He was thirty-two years old, and to all intents and purposes, completely alone in the world. He had friends, certainly, but no family of which to speak. It had occurred to him that a wife and children would ease this particular sense of aloneness, and yet he knew it was not the answer. Not for him, at any rate. He had never met a woman he wanted to marry, and he never considered his bloodline so superior that he wanted to propagate it. His work, his friends, and now Rita. That was all he needed. Good, better, best.

Ian Martin arrived shortly before seven o'clock. Rita heard his car in the drive and quickly switched off her typewriter. He would have no complaints with the work she was to deliver to her editor. She had caught up, for the most part, and if she started early in the morning, she would definitely meet her deadline.

Ian Martin was a tall and distinguished-looking man in his early fifties. A widower with married children. He carried a bottle of wine, a briefcase, and a bedraggled bouquet of daisies.

"They were fresh when I left the city." He laughed as he kissed Rita lightly on the mouth. He stood back to survey his client and felt a frown pucker his face. She was lovely, vibrant, with a new and curious glow about her. She wore her beige silk blouse open at the neck, all the way down to the shadowy cleavage between her breasts. The taupe skirt was cut slimly with a daring slash halfway up her thigh. Heeled shoes, sheer hose, and jewelry! He smiled at her a trifle nervously, wondering what she had done to herself. Where were her blue denim jeans and sweat shirt and run-down sneakers? The uniform she had adopted these last two years. He hadn't seen her looking this smart since before her divorce.

"It's good to see you, Ian. How are things back in the big city?" she asked warmly as she embraced him.

"Not much different from the last time I saw you. Life does go on in publishing. My firm has taken on several new clients, and we have great hopes for a movie deal for one of them. I also brought your last royalty statement with me. It's a good one and I banked the money for you."

Following her through the living room into the kitchen where he struggled with the cork in the bottle of wine, he was surprised when Rita turned to him, touched him on the arm and said softly, "Ian, you've been an excellent friend and business manager, but it's time for me to begin handling my own affairs."

He looked shocked, his hazel eyes narrowing as though trying to see through to her reason. Gently, she calmed him. "Ian, dear, please don't misunderstand. It is simply that I believe it's time for me to involve myself in my own finances and certainly time I involved myself in life again. I want to try my own wings." She laughed, quickly softening the statement. "Of course, I would always hope you were waiting to catch me should I begin to fall. I've become too dependent on you, and in many ways I've taken advantage of you. I don't want the time to come when you begin to resent me as a burden."

"Rita, darling," he murmured, pulling her into his embrace. "As if I could ever resent you. Surely, you know how much you mean to me. I love doing for you."

She was aware of the scent of his expensive cologne, the smoothness of his cheek as he pressed it against her brow. He must have used his battery-powered electric shaver on the drive up. Dear, fastidious Ian. So concerned with outward appearances. "Have I told you how lovely you look this evening," he said in a deep, intimate tone. "It's time you came out of that shell you built around yourself and remembered the woman you are."

Deftly, Rita extracted herself from his embrace, making a great fuss of selecting glasses for the wine. "You're right, Ian, it is time I crept out of my shell. That's one of the reasons I feel I must take over my own affairs." She meant her words to be strong, but she heard the softness in her tone, the vaguest hint of a whine and cajoling. She hated herself for it. Damn, wasn't she entitled to make her own decisions concerning the money she earned? She would like to try her hand at a little high finance, as Brett called it. Why did she always need someone to do it for her?

"Remember that tax-free fund I told you about several months back?" Ian poured the wine as he spoke; she watched the bold onyx ring on his pinky finger reflect the light. Hadn't he heard what she had said? Was he going to ignore her?

"I remember," she lied. Several months back she was hardly interested in tax-free funds or anything else, for that matter.

"The time seemed right to buy and I did. Several more opportunities like that and you'll make a handsome living just from the interest you earn."

Rita was puzzled. "How ... I mean, wasn't I supposed to sign something?"

Ian laughed, amused, as though she were a little, precocious child. "You don't have to bother your head about things like that. Remember, that's why you signed a power of attorney over to me. That tax-free fund was quite a coup, I can tell you that. ... What's the problem, Rita? Am I mistaken or did you not tell me you had no interest in financial matters?"

"No, you're right, Ian. I did tell you that." Soberly, she sipped the wine, finding it tasted acid on her tongue. She had told him she wanted nothing to do with the financial end. Suddenly, she realized why. It wasn't that she didn't consider herself capable; after all, throughout her marriage she had been the one to manage the checking account, pay the bills, sock away a little fund for vacations. No, it wasn't that she felt inadequate. After all, Ian's prestigious firm had not always been her agent. She hadn't signed with the Ian Martin Agency until she was a fully established author. In the beginning she had been the only one to decide upon contracts, payments, royalty rates, always keeping her eye on the market and delivering books that were salable and in keeping with the readers' wants and likes. She had decided whether or not she could devote periods of time, her life, actually, to fulfill a contract. And if it happened to be the wrong choice for her, she had lived with it anyway and learned from it.

Rather, her sudden dislike for finances coincided

with the trouble in her marriage. In a roundabout way she blamed her income for the distance between Brett and herself. It was almost as though she were ashamed of it. Brett had certainly made her feel that along with her increased income she had also taken to wearing the pants in the family. His words, not hers. At the end it had been such a bone of contention that she had simply turned away from such things and cheerfully deposited the responsibility with Ian.

Ian's hazel eyes blinked and his face ruddied against the stark white of his shirt collar. What had happened to the woman he had sent up here to finish her novel? He had left a trembling, insecure woman and now he found a different woman entirely. Oh, she had the same face, same name, but she wasn't the Rita Bellamy he knew, and it rankled and displeased him. Not that he ever wanted to feed on her insecurities and indecisions, but he had to admit it was certainly nice being needed and admired by an intelligent woman. Women weren't the same any longer, not since that ridiculous Women's Lib, at any rate. They all pretended to be fiercely independent, self-sufficient. What happened to those simple, endearing women who depended upon a man? Even the talented ones, like Rita, who knew their own limitations and admitted them?

Rita Bellamy was one of those old-fashioned women a man could depend on to boost his ego and see to his comforts. Maternal, loving, quietly deceptive because he knew that within her beat the heart of a very passionate woman. She stirred his blood, flattered his ego, and was so damned pretty. He liked her tremendously and would marry her if she would have him, but Rita always shied away, content to keep things on a professional level. Although there were times when he had thought she was softening to him. Like now, inviting him up to the cottage. He had even packed his silk dressing gown.

Ian had always been Rita's confidant and protector, taking care of her when the breakup in her marriage occurred. Hadn't he been the one to find her the lawyer and consult with him so that ingrate husband of hers wouldn't rake her over the coals? Now she wanted to handle her own affairs. She had no right to go and change on him, Ian's temper flared, no right at all! Taking a swallow of wine, he soothed himself. Perhaps it was only this change of life he was always reading about. Rita couldn't possibly actually mean she intended to take up the reins and make her own decisions.

"We're having broiled chicken and salad for dinner, just the way you like it," Rita called from the kitchen. "The daisies are lovely, thank you, Ian. I'll keep them near my desk to cheer me up."

"You don't appear to need cheering, darling," he told her tartly. He had thought he would spend a long evening quietly comforting her and telling her she should come back to the city as soon as her book was finished. He wished someone would comfort him; he had this strange feeling as though the rug was being pulled from under him . . . an inch at a time.

"So tell me how it's going?" He had to know what was making her look like this. He had never noticed the lilt in her voice before or the sparkle in her eyes. She had always seemed like a wounded puppy. Oh, she smiled and even laughed, but she had been so defenseless that he wanted to crush her to him and tell her it would be all right, that *he* would make it all right. That he would share his life with her. After all, their children were grown and neither of them had to account to anyone. He wondered vaguely if the ten-year difference in their ages made a difference. When he was seventy-four she would be only sixty-four.

As they sipped at the wine and made small talk, he was more than ever aware of the change in her. She was still gentle, she would always be gentle, and the sensitivity still showed, but she was different.

"When do you think you'll be coming in to the city?" Ian asked over the rim of his wineglass.

"I'm not sure," Rita said vaguely. Maybe never, she thought. Maybe when Twigg left. Maybe before. Maybe she would stay through the winter. She didn't have to make a decision now. She could drift with the days and make up her mind when she was ready. With Charles in college there was no need to rush back, and she deserved a respite between books.

"I thought your intention was to stay only till you finished the book." He tried to keep the snap and churlishness out of his voice but realized he was unsuccessful. Rita didn't notice.

"I know, but I like it here. I'm surprised, Ian, that you didn't notice my new furniture. As you can see, I'm quite comfortable here. I think I write better up here. It's certainly going well. There's nothing pressing for me back in town, and we both agreed that I wasn't going on tour for this book, so really, my time is my own. It won't cause a problem, will it?"

Her voice asked a question, but it clearly stated that she didn't care if it did make a problem.

"What about the children. The grandchildren?" Ian asked sourly.

Again, Rita failed to notice his tone. "What about them? Ian, they aren't babies. Camilla is a responsible adult and has a husband to look after her. She's a wonderful mother and she has her own friends. Even when I'm home I talk to her on the phone, but I don't see her that often. As for the grandchildren, of course, I'll miss them but they aren't my responsibility. Their mother can tend them or get a sitter. I'm sure that you must have noticed that for some reason we've grown apart lately."

"Yes, of course. It saddens me. You've always said that Camilla is closest to you, the one most like you in so many ways."

"Perhaps that's the problem. She was too much like me when we were all a family and growing. Things have changed. I've changed and Camilla has changed. She has a stepmother who is a year younger than she is. She doesn't like my career. Over the past months I've sensed that there isn't a lot Camilla does like about me. I'm sure that in her heart she blames me for the divorce. The word divorcee is not something Camilla has come to terms with. I'm sorry, but there isn't anything I can do about it. Brett forced me into this position and I intend to grow from it, not backwater and languish in an empty house. I'm just a late bloomer getting on my feet."

"Rita, you're surprising me. I've never seen this

side of you. Whatever you want is fine with me. I'm just concerned that you don't make ... make ..."

"A fool of myself? Say it, Ian. Don't talk around it and up and down it. If I do make a fool of myself over something, anything, then I'll have to take the responsibility for it. It will be my decision, my choice. I may do things wrong, make a mess of certain things, but I'll learn from my mistakes. I can live with that. Everyone else will have to live with that too."

"And Rachel and Charles?"

"Rachel is Rachel. She accepts me as I am. She has never made demands on me, and I sincerely believe she's the only one who doesn't secretly blame me for the divorce. She's been after me for over a year to 'get with it,' as she puts it. I think she'll encourage me in my independence. Charles, I'm not sure about. He still needs me, but in a limited way. He wants to know that Mom is there when he wants her. He may never physically need me, but it's important for him to know that he can at least count on me. He's going to start growing on his own now that he's in college. If we're very lucky, we can grow together. If not, one of us is going to have to take some lumps."

Ian finished the last of his wine and poured some more from the bottle. "Rita, I hardly know you any more," he said softly.

Rita smiled. Now where had she heard those words before? "I think our dinner is ready. You're a good friend, Ian. I hope you won't endanger our wonderful relationship by censoring me for *anything*. Let me try my wings. But don't catch me if they get clipped. Deal?"

What could he say? "Deal," he said morosely.

Rita chattered happily all through dinner. She might see Twigg soon. She hoped she could carry off the visit so that Ian wouldn't suspect anything. Ian was astute and tuned in. The warm feeling stayed with her when she realized she didn't really care if Ian knew. It was just that everything was so new that she wanted to keep it to herself for a while. Later, much later, she would decide if the children needed to know, and if so, how she would handle it. Probably not well, she thought with a sinking feeling in the pit of her stomach.

Rita came out of her cocoon long enough to sense there was something bothering Ian. "Is something bothering you, Ian? Something you want to talk about? I didn't mean to offend you before. I think it's time that I started doing and thinking for myself. I could have written you a letter, but I thought it would be better if we discussed it between ourselves." She didn't want him to know that she had come to this decision suddenly. As suddenly as she had decided to take Twigg for her lover. Her lover. Just the thought brought pink to her cheeks.

Ian brushed at his salt and pepper hair. He knew he was an attractive man, well groomed and polished. He had never considered women a problem for him, not even during his marriage to Dorothy. When he was younger he had to literally beat them off, and his wife, rest her soul, had never been the wiser. He wasn't a complete cad, after all. A few indiscretions, an occasional affair, but always he had been considerate of the woman who mothered his children, protecting her from any knowledge of the lapses due to his randier nature.

No, he had never had to force himself upon a woman, and it annoyed him that Rita seemed impervious to his charms. He didn't like it. At all. He stared at Rita, knowing she expected an answer of some kind. He wasn't certain he loved her. Wasn't even certain he was capable of love at his stage in life. He did know he desired her and was certain that if he could get her into bed he could please her sexually.

His feelings for Rita were more complicated than mere loving. It was something deeper, more essential to him. Need, perhaps. She made him feel needed and he responded in a basic, masculine way. The feeling that he must protect her, shelter her from hurt and disappointment, was sometimes so overwhelming it took his breath away. Together, they could live a quiet, comfortable life, mutually benefiting one another.

Over the past years he had seen flashes of this independence she was right now wearing like a badge of honor. Those times in the past they had been quickly squelched, first by Brett and later by Camilla and Charles. Guiltily, he realized he could have encouraged her to find her own strength. But he liked it when she came to him for advice and he basked in her compliments for his astute business dealings on a particular contract. Most of his other clients lived their lives in the fast lane, and they sometimes resented what they called his interference. Once a contract was signed, they didn't want to see or hear from him again unless he had a check for them.

Jesus, he didn't even like the hokey garbage

Rita wrote. But garbage or not, she was an established author with a huge following and even more potential than some of the "artists" who turned out a book once every seven years. Rita's earnings stunned him, and at times he chortled all the way to the bank. "I'm sorry, Rita, my mind was elsewhere. What were you saying?"

Rita smiled. Ian appeared tired. If Twigg didn't show up soon, Ian would go to bed and that would be the end of that. "It wasn't important. Don't feel you must stay up with me just because you're my guest. You have a long drive in the morning. I might work a little longer and since it's going good I'm getting ready to wind it down. I don't want to skip over any loose threads in the plot."

"It's the difference in our ages, isn't it? You've just realized that I'm ten years older than you are. I know you're young and vital, but I think I still have a lot of good years left in me."

Rita was about to light a cigarette. She stared at Ian, stunned at what he had just said. Her voice was brittle when she spoke. "Difference in our ages in regard to what?"

"Us. You and me."

"Ian, there is no you and me. You're my agent and I'm your client. We're friends. I didn't know that you . . . what I mean is, you never said . . . am I interpreting all of this right?"

Ian nodded. "I didn't want to rush you. The divorce and all. The children like me. You like my children. We're both grandparents. We do have a lot in common. I thought you sensed . . . perhaps, I should have spoken sooner." His voice was sober and solemn and sent a chill down Rita's spine.

"Ian, I had no idea. I'm sorry. I'm flattered, even honored, that you think of me in that way." A week ago, a month ago, she probably would have fallen into his arms and never realized that he had not mentioned the word "love."

Ian was saved from defending his statement by a knock on the door.

"Come in," Rita called happily. She wanted to laugh and throw her arms around Twigg's neck. His unruly, curly hair was still damp and clung in tight corkscrew ringlets about his face. She could smell his woodsy after-shave and it made her light-headed. For the occasion he had put on a clean, wrinkled shirt and jeans that molded his slim hips and long legs. His sneakers defied description.

"Twigg Peterson," he said, holding out his hand to Ian when he noticed Rita was just staring at him. It could have become an awkward moment.

"Ian Martin," Ian said in surprise. His eyes went to Rita and clearly said, *I thought you said no one was here but you*.

"Twigg is doing a series of articles on dolphins and killer whales. He's staying in the Johnson cottage around the bend in the lake." She wondered if Ian realized he was glaring at Twigg.

Twigg, on the other hand, had eyes only for Rita. "I'd like a beer if you don't mind. Don't get up, I can get it myself."

"Get it himself," Ian mouthed the words to Rita's smiling face. She nodded as she leaned back in her chair and lit a cigarette. Ian would never understand a man who could do for himself when a woman was around and available to do for him.

It never would have occurred to Ian to get his own beer. That's what wives and housekeepers were for.

Ian sat down heavily and Twigg returned, sitting down across from Rita and beside Ian. Rita watched the two men for a moment. With Ian's announcement and Twigg's arrival, she felt as though she were tumbling backward to square one, uncertain of herself and dreading the conversation that was to follow. Looking uncomfortable, even angry, Ian sipped his wine, draining the glass and placing it on the coffee table. His eyes shifted to Rita as though he expected her to hurry and refill it for him, or at least ask if he would care for another glass. Twigg seemed oblivious to Ian's discomfort as he drank his beer. "I managed eight hundred words today," he announced proudly.

"That's wonderful! Looks as though you're coming to terms with the assignment and it won't be long before you can put it behind you." Easily, she entered into conversation with him. With Twigg it was always so easy. Occasionally, he directed his questions to Ian who found himself joining in the light repartee.

Soon, Rita suggested that perhaps Ian might find another market for Twigg's articles, and it was the agent who expressed interest in seeing something on paper.

"It won't mean much without the pictures to accompany it," Twigg told him. "The assignment I'm doing for *National Geographic* naturally required photos, and they're damn good if I say so myself."

Ian seemed immediately interested. This was a man with high qualifications. An assignment from

National Geographic was something to boast about, and he'd heard recently that one of the major publishers was looking for subjects to print into what Ian liked to call "coffee table books."

Relieved that the two men seemed to be getting on so well despite the uncertain beginning, Rita quietly excused herself and went into the kitchen to start the dinner dishes. A little while later Twigg came in for another beer, followed by Ian carrying his empty wineglass. The conversation had now progressed to having Twigg send Ian a portfolio of his photos and text.

As though it were the most natural thing in the world, Twigg took up a dish towel and began drying as Rita washed, still continuing his conversation with Ian. If the older man was a little surprised by this action, he said nothing. When it came to business, Ian was a dynamo, and the last in the world to alienate a prospective and profitable client.

It was past midnight when Ian stood and announced he was going to bed. Rita offered to call him at five-thirty so he could beat the rush-hour traffic on Interstate 80.

"Good night, Ian," Rita said softly, refusing to meet those accusing hazel eyes that asked when, if ever, she was going to abide by propriety and send this young rascal, Peterson, home.

"Good night, dear." He kissed her perfunctorily on the cheek and warmly shook hands with Twigg. "I'll be watching for your stuff, Peterson. Don't wait too long to get it together. I have a saying 'Strike when the iron's hot.' "

"I'll do that," Twigg assured him, sitting down on the floor beside Rita's chair.

"You certainly handled him efficiently," Rita complimented after Ian had left them alone.

Twigg raised a brow. "Efficiently, is it? That's succinct and descriptive. I'll have to use that myself."

Rita laughed. Twigg knew exactly what she was talking about only he didn't think it worth discussing. Ian had been prepared to dislike Twigg and instead had offered to help him find a market for his work. Amazing. She liked the way Twigg had handled himself. Self-confident without seeming to be too brash and cocky, at least to the slightly stuffy Ian. She knew Twigg would fit into almost any group of people, being well liked as well as admired. Just look at the way he had charmed her!

Silently, Twigg drank his beer, covertly watching Rita. He wanted to drag her off to his bed, to hold her, touch her, hear her whisper his name as she tumbled over the edge of pleasure. She had lovely legs, he had noticed. Slim, gracefully turned, and teasingly revealed by the slit-hemmed skirt she wore. He had been conscious of the deep, open neck of her blouse all evening and of the shadow of cleavage it revealed. He wanted to bury his face between her breasts, breathe in the scent of her. Tenderly, her hand touched his head, running her fingers through his hair.

"Penny for your thoughts," she said softly.

Turning, he looked up into her face. "I was just thinking I'd like to throw you over my shoulder and carry you down to my cottage and make mad, passionate love to you."

For an instant, Rita's eyes glanced in the direction of Ian's room. Then, turning back to Twigg, her eyes smiled down at him. "What are you waiting for?"

His smile was dazzling, his gaze smoldering, and she was lost to her own building emotions and desires. He rose to his feet, drawing her up into his arms, dipping his face to bury it in the hollow of her throat.

Chapter Six

HE CARRIED HER INTO HIS DARKENED COTTAGE, completely sure of his movements through the darkness. Rita nestled her face into his neck, hurrying him with playful touches of her tongue against the faint stubble of tomorrow's beard. She loved the way he smelled: spicy, musky, and most of all, masculine.

I'm like a girl again, she thought, delicious tremors racing through her body. I never thought I would feel this way again, all quivery inside, a little nervous in my stomach, more than a little light-headed. She had thought those sensations were left far behind her, that a woman her age would be too old, too knowledgeable about why her blood pressure rose, to respond with any spontaneity. It wasn't so, she rejoiced. There was no such thing as "too old." Here, inside her, were those old but never forgotten feelings: the skittishness of a new colt, the wild flutter of wings, the desire, no *need,* to please and be pleasured. In his arms she was as smooth and supple as that sixteen-year-old girl within her. Her hair was as dark as walnut, her skin as white as alabaster. She felt beautiful and, feeling it, became beautiful.

He took her into his bedroom and gently placed her on his bed. She was aware of his scent in here—after-shave, soap and dampness from the adjoining bathroom, leather and tobacco. All aphrodisiacs to her senses.

Twigg flicked on the night table lamp; it glowed dimly, filling the room with a cozy glow. "I want to see you, Rita. I want to watch you when I make love to you." There was a huskiness in his voice, a seductive look in his eyes, that set her pulses racing. She watched his hands as they came down to undo the buttons on her blouse, slowly lifting it off her shoulders and kissing the newly bared flesh and the top of her breasts.

She was mesmerized by his movements, a little frightened, very much aroused. Whispers filled her head as he kissed and petted her, telling her how much she pleased him, how very much he wanted her. One by one her garments came away under his hands, and always he abated the sudden chill of skin bared to cool night air with the caress of his hands and the touch of his lips. The sound of his voice, deep, throaty, brought echoing vibrations from somewhere deep within her. She responded to him totally, entirely, allowing him to be the aggressor, the maestro.

She heard herself moaning with pleasure as his lips ignited tiny flames of fire she had thought were long cold and dead, swept like ashes in a winter wind. He was murmuring his pleasure in her, telling her she was beautiful, womanly, desirable.

Rita wanted to be beautiful for him. Wanted to bring him pleasure, make him happy. At the center of Twigg's pleasure she would find her own, waiting for her, exciting her, making her fully aware of herself as a woman. Standing before her, he began to undress. He was gold from the sun, slender and hard muscled. His chest was broad, his long arms powerful, his hips sleek and narrow. Gilt hair bloomed on his chest and threaded over his belly to thicken again in a darker grove between his thighs. His legs were long and lithely muscled, but it was to the darkness between his thighs that her eyes returned. His desire for her was evident in the proudness of his sex, and she reached out to touch him, her hands lovingly holding his maleness and falling between his thighs to that special fragility that was a man's. His hands were in her hair, his eyes closed, head thrown back on the thick column of his neck. "I love how you touch me," he told her softly, so softly, she might have only imagined he'd uttered the words.

Her arms opened to him, taking him into her embrace as he slid down into the bed, sliding his nakedness against hers and reveling in the contact between them. She was electrically charged. His mouth against hers demanded her willing response. His hands heated her flesh, finding each womanly curve and claiming them for his own. Her abandoned movements against him provoked deep sounds of delight that left him breathless. He found the roundness of her breasts and she trembled as he sought them with his mouth, kissing and teasing.

Reaching down to take him in her hand, she

stroked him, her fingers wandering to the secrets between his legs and the rough surrounding hair that so enticed her fingers. She felt the waves of bliss that emanated from him as he surrendered himself to her caress. Propping herself on an elbow, she raised herself up, tasting the freshness of his skin, nuzzling in the golden furring of his chest, trailing her lips lower, lower, until buried in the thicket surrounding his sex.

Laying back, he yielded to her, his hands never leaving her body, availing himself of the nearness of her hips, the roundness of her bottom. She captured him with her hand, drawing him to her, her mouth finding him, and she took her reward from the sound of his indrawn breath and the sudden arching of his hips.

He slid her lower body toward him, stroking the line of her back and following it over the curve of her haunches to the shadow between her thighs, parting them to avail himself of the center of her. His lips and tongue teased the sensitive flesh, his hands held her hips firmly, driving her closer to him. His mouth tasted her, devoured her, arousing echoing paroxysms in her caresses to his own body, doubling their excitement in one another, multiplying their desires.

Drawing her up beside him, he covered her mouth with his own, allowing her to taste herself on his lips, tasting himself on hers. Rita's body undulated beneath his touch as his hands strayed along her breasts, her back, between her legs. There was not an inch of her left untouched, unloved. He tantalized her, teased her, bringing her so close to the gates of her release only to deny her entrance. A fire burned in her belly and her need for him to take her grew into a hunger all-consuming. Her world was filled with him, her needs were for him alone. Only he could bring her the triumphant joy she could know as a woman.

Greedily, she took his rigid, throbbing maleness into her hand, frantically bringing it against her, rubbing it against the wetness of her yearning body. "Please, have me," she whispered, pleading, imploring, "have me now!"

He rose over her, taking her into his arms, covering her mouth with his own, his silken-tipped tongue coming in to touch and devour hers. She opened herself to him, demanding he come into her and fill this pulsing emptiness he had created within her.

He watched her face, exhilarated by the rampant lust he saw there, by the need for fulfillment she had allowed him to create within her. Lovely, so lovely. Lips parted to reveal the tip of her velvet-lined tongue; head thrown back and eyes closed with the weight of her passion. He entered her, feeling her warm, satiny sheath close and ripple around him. He wanted to bury himself in her, become a part of her, know her as he had never known another woman. Soft, kittenish sounds of pleasure fell on his ears as he moved within her, thrusting gently, becoming more insistent as his own restraint began to fail. He plunged into her, becoming one with that honeyed flesh, feeling her meet each thrust with a lift of her hips, holding fast to him with her arms, her legs, taking him deeper, wanting him deeper.

At the point of no return, Rita's eyes flew open, staring up at him, a smile lifting the corners of her kiss-bruised mouth. He felt himself falling into those clear blue depths, turning over and over, down and down, rushing toward that magical and mysterious melding of their souls that made the mating of the flesh an insignificant interlude compared to the full and total joy of loving and being loved.

Rita nestled her head against Twigg's shoulder.

"Sleepy?" Twigg murmured. Rita nodded. "I'll watch the clock for you if you want to sleep. I don't own an alarm but my watch is trustworthy."

"Hmmm," she purred contentedly, "just like you are."

"Me? Trustworthy? Why, madame, haven't you noticed that I've just ravished you?" She liked the sound of his laughter.

"You, sir, have been reading too many romances!" she pretended to scold, lightly pulling his chest hair.

"I haven't been reading romance, Rita, I've been living one. Since the day I met you." There was a deep note in his voice that started a shudder between her shoulder blades. "You, darling, are the most romantic woman I've ever known. Sweet, sensitive, womanly. Without false charades or devious facades. I like you, Rita Bellamy, very much."

His words warmed her as his embrace tightened around her, holding her close to him. He's good for me, she thought, so very good. Time spent with him was exciting and at the same time soothing. Her work was going well, and he didn't intrude himself upon her and make demands. He had work of his own, and he understood how difficult it was to restore a nebulous train of thought.

"Admit it," he whispered into the soft cloud of

her hair, "you'd completely forgotten about Ian, hadn't you?"

"Rascal! How did you know?"

"By the look in your eyes when I was making love to you. I was the only man who existed for you. Wasn't I? Admit it!" His tone was teasing, joking, but there was an underlying note prompting her confession.

"All right, I admit it. Yes, you were the only man who existed for me. You filled my world and I loved it. You touched me, Twigg, here, inside." Her hand covered her breast and her words, meant to be light and noncommittal, suddenly became her truth.

"You make me feel special," he told her, rolling over to press himself against her. His lips worshipped her breasts, the pulsing hollow of her throat, and his hands began a ritual of possession, awakening hungers she had thought satisfied. "I want to love you again, Rita. And I'm not certain I'll ever stop wanting to love you."

He took her mouth, possessed it suddenly, intently, and she felt the quickening of her response. Yes, she thought before she surrendered herself to their shared ecstasy, this is a kind of loving. If it wasn't "till death do us part," it was still a very special kind of loving.

Rita sat staring at the phone, tapping the eraser end of her pencil against her teeth. It was just after nine in the morning and Ian was long gone, sent off splendidly with a "good, old-fashioned breakfast," as he liked to call it. Coffee, bacon, eggs, juice, and a special treat of hash browned potatoes. Mountain air was invigorating, he told her as he polished off his second piece of toast and perused her typed pages.

Ian was not an admirer of historical romances, Rita knew. He considered them slightly better than trash and had once, to her horror, referred to the explicit but gently written love scenes as "soft core porn for the ladies." She had immediately set him straight on that fact, and he had never mentioned it again. He was always encouraging her to begin work on a contemporary novel, and there was a nucleus of an idea roaming around in her head. But how could he expect her to bring her head out of the seventeenth century, or thereabouts, to begin work on something modern when there was still another book due on her present contract? Impossible. Yet she had found herself dallying more and more with this particular plot line and had even sketched in some of the characters. She sighed. Perhaps after completing the next book she would take a stab at it.

Ian had not mentioned his declaration of the night before. It was painfully obvious to him that Rita was not romantically inclined in his direction. No, it would seem her interests lent themselves to much younger men. Peterson must be in his early thirties, he told himself as he gulped his coffee. He was fully aware of the fact that shortly after sending himself off to bed Rita had left the cabin with that Peterson fellow. He was already awake when she crept back into the cottage to awaken him at five-thirty as she had promised. Ian didn't care for the situation at all and believed Rita was riding for a fall. A hard fall. But he didn't suppose there was much he could do about it, unless, of course, it was affecting her work. That was why he was perusing through the pages she had delivered to him. Everything seemed to be in order, he found to his dismay. The dialogue was sharp and clean and uncluttered, and her concentration on visual description was typical Rita Bellamy, playing out the action as though it were being projected on the wide screen. Here he had been all set to gear himself up to a paternal talk with her, chastising her for her amorous activities. If Rita would no longer allow him to see to her financial affairs, he knew she would at least listen to advice concerning her work. But there was no fault to be found, and, disgruntled, he had choked down the last of his coffee and made his departure.

Rita had been glad to see him go. Ian was a dear, a good, friend, but his declaration last night and her suspicions that he knew she had not spent the night in her own bed made her uncomfortable. Go! Go! she thought. I don't want you here. I don't want anyone here. I want to explore and discover this new person I'm becoming. This new woman.

Now, sitting before the telephone, Rita had her directory opened to the number of a local gynecologist. She was being silly. She was a grown woman with three children and certainly familiar with birth control methods. But still, it all seemed too contrived. So cold and calculating.

Buck up, Rita old gal! she thought. Face it. The real dilemma comes *after* you discover you're pregnant! Use your head!

Her finger traced the line of names in the phone book. Neither she nor Twigg had spoken of birth control, but then it wasn't as though she were a sixteen-year-old schoolgirl. She was a grown woman, for God's sake, and it was natural that Twigg expected her to know how to take care of herself. Even Rachel had been on the pill since she was seventeen years old. Why, then, had it been so easy for her to come to terms with the fact that her seventeen-year-old daughter was sexually active but not with herself? Brett had always seen to that part of their relationship, using condoms or practicing coitus interruptus. Birth control was something Rita Bellamy had never given a thought to pertaining to herself. And now here she was, faced with it.

Don't be a Dumb Dora! she told herself. If a child of seventeen can think about protecting herself from an unwanted pregnancy, certainly her mother can! Almost viciously, she dialed the phone and hastily made an appointment to see the doctor. She nearly choked when she told the nurse she needed an immediate appointment, and it was for a birth control device. The voice on the other end remained cool and businesslike. God, did they always get emergency phone calls from forty-three-year-old women demanding birth control so their lovers wouldn't get them pregnant? Four o'clock. Today? Tomorrow? No, today. Rita's palms became sweaty and she could barely speak. It was unthinkable she was actually doing this! Cold. Contrived. Hell no! She finally breathed relief. The word was *smart. Adult. Responsible.*

There was a little discomfort and cramping after the insertion of the IUD, but the doctor had told her to expect it and it didn't worry her. It had occurred to Rita as she sat in the nearly empty waiting room that if she had been home in New

Jersey, no amount of frantic calling would have gotten her a same-day appointment with her own doctor. Thank heavens for small towns.

She was to refrain from sexual activity for at least twenty-four hours, the physician had said sternly, and she had felt herself blush. Did he know? Did it show that she had an ardent lover who was only thirty-two years old and very impetuous?

Twigg was coming for dinner, and Rita wondered what she would do if he wanted to make love. One did not just come out and announce to one's lover that a crazy loop of plastic had been inserted into one's vagina which was meant to prevent the embarrassment of an unwanted pregnancy and forbid one from indulging oneself that particular evening. Did one?

It was over the salad that Rita blurted out her news. Twigg sat there, fork in midair, and stared, astonished. Suddenly, he burst out laughing. Her innocence was amazing, and he was amused by it. But he was also deeply touched, for two reasons. First, that she thought enough of him to confide something so personal. Second, that he knew he was her only lover, something he had not dared ask.

Standing up, he went to her quickly, putting his arms around her and kissing the back of her neck in an impetuous gesture. "Rita, sweet, I think you're wonderful."

"Do you? Even though I sit here and confess my naivete, I'm having growing pains, Twigg, and they hurt. I've been so protected all my life, and now I know I must face the fact that I'm a grown woman and accept responsibility for it."

"That's what's so wonderful. That you'll let me stand around to watch and share it with you."

Later that night, when all the world should have been asleep, Twigg held her in his arms, smoothing his hands over her naked body and just holding her. They talked, they laughed and shared secrets. They touched and caressed and kissed, but the fires of their passions were banked and kept to softly glowing embers. She knew he wanted her, he told her so, and the hard evidence of his desire was pressed between her legs. She learned there were other and very meaningful ways to express tenderness and passion without the act of intercourse. And all of them left her cheeks pink and lips ruddy and feeling completely loved. Twigg's brand of loving.

It was late in the afternoon when Rachel pulled up the driveway, horn blaring to herald her arrival. Rachel never did anything without noise and fanfare, and the more the better, Rita smiled to herself. Only that morning Rachel had called to say she was making a "surprise" visit before she winged off to Miami with "whatziizname."

Rita clicked off her typewriter when she heard the MG sports car in the drive. She enjoyed Rachel's outrageous company, and while she might secretly disapprove of some parts of the girl's lifestyle, she would never condemn her own child.

Rachel was a striking young woman, sable-haired and model-thin, with soft feminine curves in only the right places. The slinky blouse and the painted-on jeans with designer label made Rita's eyes bulge. How did she walk and bend in them? Carefully, Rachel giggled.

"How goes it, Mummy dear? Slaving away in the boonies with no one but the chipmunks to keep you company?" Not waiting for a reply, she asked, "What's for dinner? Spaghetti. I knew it. It smells delicious, as always. I could eat spaghetti seven days a week."

Rita poured two glasses of orange juice, wondering if she was pleased that Rachel had decided at the spur of the moment to come up to the lake. Worse, and contrary to all she thought maternal, she wondered exactly how long her daughter intended to stay. Not that she would ever ask her to leave. Everything would simply have to be put on a back burner for the present, or at least while Rachel was here. Everything included Twigg. Rita wasn't ready to reveal that relationship to her offspring, if she ever would be, not even to high-flying, free-winging Rachel.

Mother and daughter were settled next to the fireplace sipping their juice. "I really love what you've done to the cottage, Mum. Did you have a decorator come in and do it for you? It's a glad and far cry from your usual stuffy choices, Mum. Did I ever tell you I never liked chintz and antiques and overstuffed chairs? And I always hated those ridiculous tester beds you had in the room Camilla and I shared at home."

Rita looked blankly at her child. She had always thought she had furnished their home with love and comfort. A fine time to discover that her child had never appreciated the furnishings and had actually hated the beautiful antique beds she had refinished and stained especially with her daughters in mind. Rachel was so opinionated, had always been, even as a child, and Rita couldn't help but wonder what else Rachel had disliked and hated while she was growing up. Something else to go on the back burner, she supposed, deciding not to pursue the subject. But it hurt terribly, to know that her efforts had not been appreciated. "How is everything, Rachel? Have you seen Camilla and the children?"

"Mother, you know Camilla is pissed with me. I knew you were going to ask, so when I stopped for gas on the way up here, I called her from a phone booth. She was cool, very cool. I asked about the monsters and she said they were fine. Tom is fine. The dog is fine. What that means is the dark stuff hit the fan when you refused to baby-sit. Not to worry. Camilla will come around. She has to pout first. I'm surprised at you, Mum, Camilla was always your favorite, you should know how she does things."

"Rachel, that's not true. I have no favorites among my children. I've never shown favoritism and you know it."

"Mum, it doesn't matter. We're each our own person. Camilla is a dud. Charles has potential, if you don't smother him. Daddy, well, Daddy wanted something and he went for it. Now you, Mother, are another brand of tea."

"When are you leaving for Miami?" Rita asked, trying to change the subject. It was because Camilla was the oldest. A parent sometimes felt something special for the firstborn. It didn't mean the other children were loved any less.

"Tomorrow, the plane leaves at five-ten. I'll be back Monday morning. Mom, they picked my designs for the new trade show. A hefty bonus. That means I can start paying you back. Will one hundred fifty dollars a month be okay to start? If I pick up the top prize, I can pay you back in one lump sum."

"Fine. Whenever. Don't cut yourself short. You know I was glad I could help you. More than that I'm proud of you and appreciate your effort to repay me. Have you seen your father?"

"No. But I talked to him a week or so ago. He doesn't call. I do my duty and try to call once every ten days or so. He really has nothing to say to me. I think he's embarrassed. I asked him if he heard from Charles and he said no. Camilla calls him every day and makes sure the kids get on the phone. I just know Daddy is thrilled to be reminded that he has three grandchildren when he just married a twenty-two-year-old chick."

"Rachel, that's no way to talk about your father."

Rachel's wide, blue eyes were innocent. "Why?"

"I really don't want to go into it now. Why don't you take a walk around the lake or go outside and rake some leaves for me? I want to finish something I'm working on, and then we'll have dinner. We can spend the evening together. Ian was here and he brought me some new books."

"Sounds good to me, Mummy. Are you cooking the long spaghetti or the shells?"

"Shells. Two boxes of them so I can put on another five pounds." Rita grinned.

"You *are* getting a little hefty. Must be all this good clean living up here. You just sit and work and then sit and eat, right? That'll do it. You're at that age where it all goes to the middle. You should give some thought to working it off. Join an exercise class! It's bad enough being a grandmother at forty-three, but a fat grandmother is a no-no. By the way, I think you need a touch-up. You don't want to be a fat and gray-haired grandmother. I'll do it for you tonight, if you like. Okay?"

Rita nodded as she sucked in her stomach. "Dinner is in an hour. Don't get lost."

"That's what you used to say when I was a kid. How can I get lost? This place is about as big as a penny and I know it like the back of my hand. Listen, I saw smoke coming out of the Johnson chimney. Are they here?"

Rita swallowed hard. "No, they have a tenant." Leave it to Rachel; don't ask questions, she prayed. She turned her back on her daughter and clicked on the IBM. Her shoulders were tense as she tried to work with her stomach sucked in.

Two hours later Rita glanced down at her watch. Rachel should have been back by now. It was almost dark outside. From the bedroom window she had a clear view of the lake and the Johnson cottage. She would not spy. She would not look out that window to look for her daughter.

Bustling into the kitchen, she busied herself with the sauce and setting the table, laying out napkins, putting water on to boil for the macaroni. She cleaned the coffeepot and measured out coffee. Mixed a salad and slit the Italian garlic bread and stuck it in the oven, only to take it out again. Where was Rachel?

Another half hour crawled by as Rita drank two cups of steaming coffee. She would not spy. She could throw open the front door, walk out onto the deck, and shout Rachel's name as she had when Rachel was a child. No, she wouldn't do that either. Rachel was all grown, a woman, used to making her own choices and decisions.

Unconsciously, she sucked in her gut and marched into the living room. She felt angry. And guilty. What if Rachel had walked up to the Johnson cottage and knocked on the door and introduced herself? That was Rachel's style. What if they were both inside, laughing and talking? What if Rachel was telling tales about her childhood, making it perfectly obvious to Twigg that Rita was really too old for him? Rachel was spontaneous and charming and totally disarming.

This is ridiculous! Rita snapped to herself. Twigg knows exactly how old I am ... no, that wasn't what was eating her. The truth was, she felt threatened by her own daughter who was young and lovely. And her maternal pride was prompting her to think Rachel was everything and more a man like Twigg would find to his tastes.

Chapter Seven

THE FRONT DOOR OPENED AND RACHEL WALKED IN, Twigg behind her. Rita's heart flopped and then righted itself. She forced a smile to her lips. "Hello, Twigg. I see you've met my daughter."

"I've invited him for dinner, Mother. He said you were friends so I didn't think you would mind. When you make spaghetti, you make lots. Twigg was sitting on his front porch when I walked by. He thought I was you. I don't know how he could have made such a mistake." She laughed, a derisive note in her tone. "I don't *look* anything like you!" Rita sucked in her stomach again.

"That's nice. I hope you like spaghetti, Twigg." How brittle and dry her voice sounded.

"Love it." Did his voice sound apologetic? Again, Rita tucked in her stomach.

"Can I get either of you something? I have a few more things to do in the kitchen. Coffee, beer, wine?"

"Nothing for me," Twigg said quietly.

"Me neither, Mummy. I was telling Twigg about your grandchildren on the way over. Tell him I didn't lie, that they really are called 'the monsters.'"

"They're mischievous, like most children," Rita said defensively. Why did she have to call her a grandmother in front of Twigg? *Because,* an inner voice responded, *she doesn't know you slept with him, and she is only saying what she would say under any circumstance. You're nitpicking, Rita.*

She attacked the salad greens with a vengeance as she chopped and sliced them into a large wooden bowl. She wondered what they were talking about in the living room. It sounded too quiet. Knowing Rachel as well as she did, it didn't have to mean they were talking. They could be doing other . . . She sucked in her stomach again as she bent down to take the garlic bread from the oven. She set it on a rack to cool before slicing. Waiting impatiently for the pasta to boil, she had a feeling she wasn't going to enjoy dinner. Rachel was so young and beautiful. God, she couldn't be jealous of her own child, could she?

She called them for dinner and sat down. Twigg was opposite her, and Rachel was at the end of the table.

Rita picked at her dinner not wanting to eat the heavy pasta. She stirred the salad around on her plate and ate a piece of lettuce from time to time as she listened to Rachel and Twigg talk about the tennis match at Forest Hills. "As far as I'm concerned, Borg has great form, do you agree?" Twigg nodded as he wolfed down the meal.

"I think Connors has about had it—he's such a show-off. Mother, you aren't eating, how come?

Don't tell me I really got to you with that business of getting too fat. I was just teasing you."

Twigg stared across at Rita, his eyes wide and thoughtful, even puzzled. She hadn't said much, not that her loquacious daughter gave her much of a chance. "How did the writing go today? I don't mind telling you I had a hard time," he said enthusiastically. "I have to admire you, the way you can string words together. Two words at one time is okay, but give me three or four and I have to rewrite."

"It will get easier as you go along. Don't be so quick to discard what you write. Usually, the first thing you do is the best. You just spin your wheels after that. That's the way it works for me, anyway."

Rachel stared from her mother to Twigg. A glimmer of comprehension appeared in her wide-eyed gaze. Her mother was uncomfortable. Twigg was at ease and concerned with Rita's silence. He was going out of his way to include her in the dinner conversation. And the way he got up and opened the refrigerator, as though he knew just where everything was.

Hating to be ignored, Rachel interrupted the conversation. She was aware that her mother was annoyed with her and that Twigg had forgotten she was there. "How long are you staying at the lake, Twigg?" Rachel asked pointedly.

"I'm not sure," Twigg replied evasively.

"Mother?"

It took Rita several moments until she realized the one word was a question.

"I haven't definitely decided. It depends on how soon I finish and if there are going to be any further rewrites. There's no reason for me to hurry back with Charles away at college."

"But, Mother, it's going to be getting cold. You don't like the mountains in the winter. You know how you like to snuggle in with your woolly bathrobe early in the evening."

Rita almost laughed as she met Twigg's eyes. His bright green gaze said he could offer other ways to keep warm.

Rachel felt her eyes narrow. "You won't mind then if I come up to keep you company after the trade show, will you? I'll have some time off before I have to get back into the swing of things. It's the week of Charles's big game."

It was on the tip of Rita's tongue to say yes, she *did* mind, she minded *very much*! If there was one thing Rachel had never done, that was to spend more than one day in her mother's company, becoming definitely antsy to get back to the city and her own life-style. She shrugged. "If I'm still here, of course you can come up. However, you don't like the mountains in the winter either."

"Mother, how can you say that! I ski every winter. Do you ski, Twigg?"

"Some," Twigg answered as he pushed his plate away. "I go to Tahoe a couple of times a year. Do you ski, Rita?"

Rachel laughed. "Mother ski! Mummy's idea of exercise and sports is to watch it on TV. Right, Mother?"

Rita forced a smile to her lips. Rachel couldn't be doing this deliberately, or could she? The thought of the two snowmobiles she had bought on impulse anticipating wondrous hours of her and Twigg skimming over the snow nearly choked her.

Her tone was light, casual, when she replied. "Rachel's right. I'm a creature of comfort. I don't do any of the things you *young* people do." She bit back the urge to mention her secret of the snow-mobiles. "Why don't you take your coffee and go into the living room. I'll clear away here and join you when I'm finished."

"I'll help you, Rita. It's the least I can do after such a good dinner."

"I can see you don't know Mom very well. If there's one place you stay away from, it's her kitch-en. C'mon, we'll do what she wants. If you leave them we can do them later, Mother, while I'm dyeing your hair," Rachel called over her shoulder.

"I changed my mind, Rachel. I decided I like the little bit of gray I have. Go along, I can finish up here."

Twigg's eyes frantically sought hers in apology for the second time. Rita smiled before she turned to the sink to run the water.

The minute the door closed behind them, Rita wanted to smash something. Hot, scorching anger engulfed her. She couldn't ever remember being so angry. Angry at herself, angry at Rachel. But never angry with Twigg.

Rita washed and dried the dishes slowly, delay-ing the time when she would have to go back into the living room. She cleaned the coffeepot and got it ready for the morning. She carried out the trash and put a new liner in the waste basket. She swept minuscule crumbs from the floor and then washed off the dustpan; she didn't know why she did it. She looked at the yellow plastic scoop and grimaced. Who ever heard of washing a dustpan? There was nothing else to do but light a cigarette. So far she had killed thirty-seven minutes.

She almost bumped into Twigg when she pushed the swinging door that led to the living room. He was so near, so close, she thought she could hear the beat of his heart. It was probably her own. "Sorry," she muttered.

"I've got to be going, Rita. I want to transcribe some tapes and I promised myself an early start in the morning. Thanks for dinner." He squeezed her shoulder intimately before he left. Rachel waved good-bye and Rita walked to the door and opened it for him. "Good night, Twigg."

"See you tomorrow."

"See you tomorrow," Rachel mocked after the door closed. "Mother, is something going on here I don't know about?" Not waiting for a reply to her ridiculous question, she rushed on. "He's fascinating. Wouldn't you know I had to come to the woods to find a really titillating man. He's not married either. How old would you say he is, Mom?"

"In his early thirties I would imagine."

"Just right." Rachel grinned. "If you're serious about not dyeing your hair, I think I'll turn in. I'm beat. Don't forget to wake me early. Night, Mom."

"Good night, Rachel."

Rita walked back to the kitchen for a wineglass and a bottle of wine. She sat in front of the fire drinking steadily. He skied, he played tennis. He was thirty-two. He didn't take vitamins with extra iron like she did. He was lean and fit. He was only a few years older than her children. He was young.

God, thirty-two was so young. A set of tennis would kill her. Skiing would make her a basket case.

Rita nursed the bottle of wine until she was tipsy. "Drunk!" she admitted rebelliously. Her last conscious thought before she fell into bed fully clothed was that it wasn't fair. Nothing about any of this was fair—from Twigg, to Ian, to Rachel, to herself.

It was early morning; Rita could tell from the filtered light coming in between the drawn drapes. She half heard Rachel when she poked her head into the room to announce, "It's a good thing I have my own built-in alarm or I would still be out. See you soon, Mother. I'll call you when I get back from Miami."

"Regards to Patrick," Rita mumbled as she slid beneath the covers.

"Who? Oh, Patrick. Right! See you, Mom. Say good-bye to Twigg for me."

The golden idyllic days of autumn were upon them. October had fulfilled the promise of an Indian summer—warm, balmy days and cool, crisp nights. The landscape became a tapestry of golds, oranges, and reds, wild and abandoned color to match the abandon of Rita's emotions.

Her novel was completed and she knew it was good. Via Ian, it had been sent to the copy editor with no revisions due. Time was her own and she reveled in it. Until the first of the year she had only to research and set up her next outline.

Twigg was still busy with his project and hoped to be finished before Christmas. Christmas! Had another year rolled nearly to the end? Neither of them could believe it. Had it only been just after Labor Day that they had met? Only weeks ago, really. How had they come to know one another so well, learned so much about the other? Concentration, Twigg had laughingly said.

Writing was new to him. Theses and papers published through the university came easily enough, writing for an audience of students and biologists already quite familiar with his subject of marine life. However, preparing for a larger, less informed audience was totally different, and he had come to depend upon Rita to review his work, encouraging her to be free with her criticism and she was, boldly. Her point of view was valuable to him, and she would not diminish it with flattery instead of honesty. Recognizing this, Twigg followed her advice where she suggested he clarify certain passages.

Rita liked helping him this way, instinctively knowing he never would have asked if she were still busy with work of her own. It was another side of their relationship and their growing dependence upon one another, and she enjoyed it immensely.

She was learning she could allow herself to be dependent upon Twigg for companionship and fun and a sharing of interests. Yet it was a new kind of dependency that required nothing of her, only her desire to be with him and he with her. There was none of the feeling that he might begin directing her life, press his opinions upon her, or try to protect her the way Ian had done. And when her opinion differed from his, there was none of the bitter derision there had been with Brett. With Twigg, Rita could be together with him, feel he was a part of her life and she of his, and yet remain an entity herself.

The day after Rachel's departure, Rita had contemplated her life. She had thought about Twigg, her children, and her grandchildren, but, mostly, she had thought about herself. This alone was a breakthrough as far as she was concerned. Too often for too many years she had shirked the effort of coming to know herself the way she was today, now, instead of remembering herself as she had been twenty years before when her role in life was clear-cut and simple. Wife and mother.

She attempted to decide if a diet and weight loss would make her happy. If so, would she be doing it for herself or for Twigg's approval? Then she made the decision to diet and watch her weight because it was what *she* wanted. Her cigarette habit was consciously cut in half, going down to less than a pack a day and switching to a low tar brand. Soon, with effort and willpower, she planned to kick the habit altogether. She lived with her decisions for several days before she started her new routines, wanting to be certain she was comfortable with what she was doing. She made no mention of it to Twigg nor to her children when she spoke with them on the phone. She believed her decisions were wise and healthful and would benefit her in the end.

It was Twigg who invited her to come jogging with him, and at first she demurred, claiming it was too rigorous. But she did take walks, long ones, while he worked on his articles, and she liked the fresh bloom of color that was returning to her cheeks. Often, when he noticed her through his window, he would join her, silently urging her to quicken her pace. Now, four weeks later, she was actually jogging with him a quarter way around the lake and seeing her reward on the bathroom scale.

The pretense of separate living quarters had been abandoned by mutual consent. Twigg used the Johnson cottage for work and had moved into Rita's cottage with her.

It was delicious waking in the morning and finding herself in his arms. It was heaven to no longer eat dinner alone. Reading, watching TV, or just sitting by the fire talking, everything was wonderful with Twigg.

Their lovemaking had reached new heights of intimacy and freedom. He encouraged her to be the aggressor when the mood struck her, and yet he never took her for granted. His delight with her seemed to increase and take on new colorations. His lusty demands in bed left her feeling desirable and every inch a woman. He told her he couldn't get enough of her and proved it by his ardor and attention.

They had gone into the city together three times. Once for Rita to lunch with her publicist and twice for Twigg to meet with Ian and an interested publisher. Each time Rita had seen and appreciated another side of him. She liked the way he put people at their ease, thoroughly enjoying their conversation and learning about their interests outside their work. He fit in. Simply put, but true. The young female publicist had winked surreptitiously at Rita, and the publisher, known to be a hard-nosed, opinionated man, had been charmed by him. Twigg easily won respect and a handsome publishing contract into the bargain.

Rita poured another cup of coffee when she saw Twigg running up the path after a morning's work. "You're invited to dinner tonight," he told her, carefully sipping the steaming brew. "My place around six. Nothing special, steaks and salad, I suppose. I'll run into town and pick everything up. I'm having some guests, good friends of mine, and I know you'll enjoy them." Suddenly his eyes locked with hers, concern wrinkling his brows. "You will come, won't you? It's short notice and I know my cooking isn't the best . . ."

Rita laughed delightedly. "Of course I'll come," she assured him, rewarded by his smile. Inwardly, there was a note of alarm. She wasn't quite certain she was ready to share him with his friends or to have their solitude invaded. Because of this, she had tried to keep her own children away, and in Camilla's case it was met with sullen disappointment.

"You'll like them, both of them. They live in New York and they'll probably stay the night because we're known to stay up to the wee hours talking. It's sort of a celebration for the publishing contract. Both of them are eager to meet you, especially Samantha, who proclaims herself to be your most ardent fan."

"You've told them about me?" she said weakly.

"Of course. You're my lady, Rita, and very important to me. I want my friends to meet you, to know you. I would be selfish to keep you all to myself." His hand reached over the table, capturing hers. "They're very good friends, and very discreet. I promise you. But if you're uneasy about meeting them or having them know about us, I'll call them back and tell them it's off." He spoke quietly but without a trace of judgment. He was simply concerned for her feelings and would sacrifice an evening with his friends if it was what she wanted.

Feeling terribly selfish and yet somehow proud that he had admitted to his relationship with her, Rita grasped his fingers and squeezed. "You're very sweet, Twigg, and terribly sensitive to my feelings and I appreciate it. Truly. Certainly I want to meet your friends, especially if one of them is a fan."

"Samantha said she was getting all her books together to have you autograph them." He laughed. "You'll find her somewhat exuberant but altogether charming. Is there anything I can get for you in town? Would you like to come with me?"

"No, on both counts. If you're going to have guests, I'd better give my hair a wash. I can't disappoint my public, you know."

Twigg kissed her soundly, telling her they'd have time for their walk when he came back from town. Then, in a teasing and seductive voice, he said, "Of course, if you can think of some other kind of exercise while I'm gone, I want you to know I'm open to suggestions."

A delicious shiver ran up her spine. It was heaven being wanted by this man, and she was drunk with the power of her own sensuality.

After he left, Rita allowed herself to frown into her coffee cup. She was presented with the problem of what to wear that evening. Slacks, skirt, jeans? If she knew who these friends were, how old they were, she would know what to wear. There it was again, the age problem. She had every reason to suppose that Twigg's friends were as young as he, younger even. And the name

Samantha brought to mind a young, slim girl with long blond hair and not much on her mind. That was unfair! And ridiculous! Here she was picturing a flower child of the sixties just because of the name Samantha. If Twigg had thought his friends would not like her or that she would be uncomfortable with them, he never would have invited them up to the lake. You've got to begin trusting, Rita, my dear, she chastised herself, both yourself and others.

At five after six Rita knocked on the door to the Johnson cottage. Twigg's friends had arrived, she knew. Their car was parked beside his in the drive. She could hear the sound of voices from within. Earlier that afternoon, Twigg had returned from town and they had taken their walk. When she offered to help him with dinner or straightening the cottage, he had refused, telling her to take the time to make herself beautiful. After a long leisurely bath Rita had decided upon gray slacks and a bulky turtleneck sweater of banded pastel colors from beige to pink to lavender. Her chestnut hair gleamed in soft, collar-length waves, and she carried a bottle of Twigg's favorite wine. It had taken all of her courage to overcome her sudden shyness and actually walk the path to his cottage.

Twigg himself opened the door, smiling approvingly at her and kissing her lightly in thanks for the presented wine. He made informal introductions to Eric and Samantha Donaldson.

"You've seen Eric on the six o'clock news, Rita. That's why he looks so familiar. Samantha used to teach pottery and ceramics at the university; that's how I came to know them."

Immediately, Rita was brought into their fold.

Eric was a handsome man, dressed casually in slacks and a hand-knit sweater, and when she commented on it, Samantha smilingly took the credit.

Samantha, Rita was glad to see, was a far cry from the "flower child" she had envisioned. A tall, slim woman with Titian hair and an obvious flare for fashion, Rita liked her immediately because of her charming smile and warmth.

"I'm so pleased to meet you," Samantha said brightly, without gushing as so many did when meeting a renowned novelist. "I so enjoy your work and want you to know it."

Rita was pleased to know this stylish and graceful woman liked her work. She spied several of her older titles on the coffee table and remembered what Twigg had said about Samantha wanting them autographed.

"Twigg has been telling us about you," Eric supplied, smoothing a hand over his iron-gray hair. "He admires you greatly."

"That's my stuffy, news commentator husband for you, Rita." Samantha smiled. "We've been looking forward to meeting you since Twigg first told us about you, and you're everything he said you were." There was an embarrassed moment. What had Twigg told them? How much had he said? Twigg slipped his arm around her shoulders, pulling her against him, easing the awkward moment.

"We're going to sit right here while the *men* fix the dinner," Samantha announced. "If you need help, don't call us, call Betty Crocker," she told them as she pointed them in the direction of the kitchen. "And whatever you do, do it quickly. I'm starved!"

Sitting beside Samantha, Rita felt herself relax.

Samantha was a friendly and talkative woman, enthusiastic and knowledgeable. It wasn't long before they were discussing acquaintances they had in common in New York and favorite recipes for spaghetti sauce. As an artist in ceramics, Samantha was familiar with the antique pottery Rita collected and was impressed with the author's knowledge of early American pottery houses.

"It was something I stumbled upon while doing research for one of my books," Rita explained. "I found myself intrigued and began a modest collection. However, I must admit I frequent a shop in the city and pick up pieces from a favorite potter of mine. The name is Jeffcoat, and I particularly like the banded shades of blue she uses and the mottled browns. Have you ever heard of her?" she asked Samantha.

"Heard of her!" Eric laughed as he came from the kitchen carrying a tray with two glasses of wine. "You are speaking to Samantha Jeffcoat Donaldson. Jeffcoat is Samantha's maiden name."

"How trite that sounds," Samantha complained. "Maiden name, posh! It's my name, sweetheart. Donaldson is your name! You distinguish yours and I'll distinguish mine!"

Everyone laughed when Eric complained some of Sam's brainstorms were right out of the pages of *Ms.* magazine. "Except the floor wax advertisements and laundry powder ads. Sam does discriminate against anything to do with household chores," he said good-naturedly.

"Oh, hush, Eric, I want Rita to stroke my ego by telling me how she loved my work! It will make me feel so much better about asking her to autograph her books for me and allow me to present her with that little hand-thrown bowl I've brought along for her!"

Dinner was delicious and afterward Twigg threw more logs on the fire and they all congregated near the hearth. There was an unforced camaraderie, and they all basked in one another's company. Eric and Sam were easy people, sensitive and discerning. Listening to them speak on a wide range of subjects and enthusiastically offering her own opinions and having them respected was good for her ego. But it was when Eric and Sam asked after some friends they had left behind on the west coast that Rita realized Twigg traveled in a varied circle of people. Some of them artists, some in the media, academics and even what Sam called "Hollywood types." Twigg made eclectic choices in his friendships, and yet their varied backgrounds seemed to blend harmoniously in his life. Apparently, somewhere, there were "flower children" with whom he associated, but he did not restrict himself to types when it came to making relationships.

It was nearly three in the morning when Rita made a move to leave, and the Donaldsons begged off to go to bed. Twigg walked her back to the cottage and kissed her warmly at the front door. "I told you you would like them. And they adore you, especially Eric. I saw the approving glances he was throwing at you all evening. I should be jealous, but I'm not. I know Samantha is the only woman for him."

Returning his kiss, Rita expected him to return to his cottage, but he opened her door and stepped in behind her. He took her into his arms. "I love you like this, all sleepy and warm from the conversation and the wine. I want to make love to you, Rita Bellamy, and then I'm going to hold you in my arms all night long." And he made good on his promise and never once did Rita worry what the Donaldsons were thinking when Twigg didn't return.

Chapter Eight

THE DAYS SLID BY, EACH MORE BEAUTIFUL AND wonderful than the day before. Two and a half months had passed since she had met Twigg Peterson. Two and a half months that were probably the happiest of her life.

It was ten days before Thanksgiving and Charles's important football game. Rita had promised to attend and attend she would. Somehow, she had managed to lose ten pounds and had also whittled off several inches in crucial areas. Her breathing was less labored because she had cut her smoking in half. One of these days she hoped she could give it up entirely. But not yet.

The only blight on her happiness was that Twigg would be leaving the day after Christmas. She knew she would have to deal with that when the time came.

Rita got up, stretched luxuriously, and then added more logs to the fire. It felt like snow. It even looked like snow. She hoped so. She had never been marooned before and would enjoy it. It was a known fact that this area of the Poconos was the last to see a snowplow, and it was not unheard-of to remain snowbound for as long as four or five days.

The phone rang, jarring her from her thoughts. "Hi, Mother. It's Rachel. I'm calling to make sure you're still in residence. If you want I'll bring the turkey. Talk to me, Mum."

"Yes, I'm here, Rachel. It feels like snow so you better bring your boots and warm clothing. When are you planning on coming up? I appreciate your offer, but I'll take care of the turkey."

"Thursday. I'll stay through the weekend after Thanksgiving. By the way, is your handsome neighbor still there? If it snows, maybe we could go skiing together."

Rita drew in her breath. "Yes, he's still here. I'm not sure if he has skis. Perhaps you should bring Charles's if that's what you want to do."

"Good thinking, Mum. Okay, see you Thursday."

Rita replaced the phone. She could have told Rachel not to come, that she was knee-deep in work. That she couldn't holiday on Thanksgiving and lose time if she intended to be at Charles's game the next day. Why hadn't she? The question punished her, demanding she admit the truth. "Because," she blurted aloud, "because I'm challenging Twigg to find my young, vivacious daughter more desirable than me. I'm testing him and I hate myself for it, but God help me that's what I'm doing."

Now she was in a funk. All the old insecurities flooded through her. All the old guilts. And jealousy. She was jealous of her own daughter. Twigg had been more gallant after Rachel's last visit. Neither of them had discussed her child and her tactless comments concerning Rita. As long as she was keyed on self-destruct she might as well call Camilla and then Charles.

Rita waited patiently while Camilla quieted the children. "Mother, I can't believe what you're telling me. Are you saying Charles's football game is more important than spending Thanksgiving with your grandchildren? I spoke to Rachel last night, and she said she was going up to see you and said there was the most interesting man there that she wanted to get to know better. Why is it always Rachel, Mother?"

"Camilla, I promised Charles when he started the semester that if he made the team I would go to the Thanksgiving game. I can't go back on my word. Surely, you can understand how important it is to your brother."

"Are you planning on leaving Rachel there at the cottage with the new, interesting man? Mother, I can't understand you anymore. You seem to have changed. Anything goes, anything Rachel does, no matter how outrageous it is, is okay with you. Mother, ever since you started that . . . that career of yours, you've . . . never mind. I think you should know that Daddy is going to the game too. He's probably going to take Melissa. Are you sure you're ready for that?"

Rita cringed. Not at the words but at Camilla's bitchy tone. "As ready as I'll ever be," Rita said, forcing a light note into her voice.

"You're so different, Mother. Everything is so different. I'm sorry if I sound like I'm ticked-off.

You don't seem to care anymore. Do you realize you've been gone for almost four months. We've missed you, especially the kids."

"I didn't call you so we could get into a hassle. I wanted you to know about Thanksgiving in plenty of time. Besides, Camilla, this year it's your turn to have dinner with Tom's family. Maybe you think I've forgotten, but I haven't. This is your year for Christmas with Tom's family too."

"Mother, does that mean you aren't coming back for Christmas?" Camilla shrieked.

"I'm not sure. More than likely, I'll stay here. Charles will want to come here so he can do some skiing. We have plenty of time for all of that. I hesitate to remind you, but you do have a father."

"Oh, Mother, he's so wrapped up in Melissa, he has no time either. The whole family is falling apart. Rachel is so flaky and you never know where or what she's going to be doing from one minute to the next. Charles is away and he never writes or calls. I feel so alone."

"Camilla, you have your own life, your own little family, and it's going to be whatever you make it. I'll always be here if you need me, but I do have my own life to lead, and I intend to lead it the way I see fit. I won't allow you or Rachel or Charles to dictate to me."

"All you think about is your books, your royalty statements, and your super-duper business deals. You have no time for us anymore, Mother."

"That's not true, Camilla. What you mean is I'm not at your beck and call anymore. You also resent that I now do something other than housework. That I've become my own person and am no longer an extension of your father."

"There's no point in discussing this anymore. I can see I can't get anywhere with you. Do you want to speak to the kids?"

"I'd love to talk to them if they aren't screaming and crying. I can't see paying long-distance rates for me to listen to you yell at them and then all they do is scream more."

"Forget it, Mother, just forget it. Tom isn't going to believe this. Oh, yes, he will, he still remembers the last conversation he had with you. Good-bye, Mother."

"Give my regards to Tom and the children. Good-bye Camilla."

One ten-minute conversation with Camilla was enough to drain one's life's blood. Now, for Charles.

Rita listened to some good-natured banter while she waited for Charles to come to the phone. "Hey, Bellamy, there's some chick on the phone for you" made her grin from ear to ear. She had to remember to tell Twigg.

"Charles, it's Mom. How are you?"

"Mom, wow, why are you calling? Is something wrong?"

"Good heavens, no. I just wanted to see if you were all right and if you got your allowance."

"Got it and spent it. The guys had a beer party and I had to put in my share. I'm okay. Hey, you still coming up for the game?"

"I'll be there, you can count on it."

"Uh, Mom, you do know Dad is coming, don't you? Do you think it will be a problem? I think he's bringing Melissa. I didn't know what to do so I just sort of ignored the whole thing."

"I think we're all adult enough to handle it."

"There is something I need to talk to you about."

Need. He had said *need*. He needed her. How different he sounded. How grown up. "Yes, Charles, what is it?"

"With the situation between you and Dad as it is, I thought there might be a problem about Thanksgiving dinner. About who to have dinner with, I mean. So what I thought I'd do was accept an invitation to Nancy Ames's house for dinner. She doesn't live far from here, and she said I could bring you along. What do you think, Mom?" he asked anxiously.

Oh, God, oh, God, her baby was worrying about her. He was making decisions for himself and for her. He cared about her feelings being hurt.

"I think that's wonderful, but you go alone. Rachel is coming up to the cottage for Thanksgiving so I won't be alone. I was worried about you. Is Nancy your girl?"

"Almost. I haven't clinched it yet. You know, given her my high school ring. I'm working on it though. Do you think it would be all right if I brought her up to the cottage the weekend after Thanksgiving?"

"I sure do. I'd like to meet her." She suddenly wanted to see Charles share his happiness and his new sense of himself.

"One more thing, Mom. Is Dulcie still staying in the house, or did you let her go when you moved to the cottage?"

"No, she's still at the house. Someone had to stay there to make sure the pipes don't freeze. Charles, I didn't move to the cottage; I'm only staying here between books. Why did you want to know?"

"Do you think she could make me a batch of

brownies and send up my gray sweat suit? Ask her if she'll fish around for my Izod socks, the black and gray ones."

Rita smiled. "Charles, I have some free time, I could make the brownies for you."

"Thanks, Mom, but I think I'd rather have Dulcie's. No offense."

"None taken."

"What time do you think you'll get to the game?"

"Just about game time if the weather is okay. Do you need anything else?"

"Nope, that about covers it."

"Okay, I'll see you a week from tomorrow."

"Bye, Mom."

She felt pleased with herself when she hung up the phone. Charles was going to be okay. Nancy, whoever you are, you have my blessing and my thanks. Her baby worried about her. It was wonderful. Everything was wonderful. Well, *almost* everything; the thought of her daughters popped into her mind.

Twigg arrived back at Rita's cottage, his face glowing with excitement like a small boy's. "Have you looked outside?" At her bewilderment, he led her away from her desk where she was making notes for her next book and brought her to the panoramic windows in the living room. "Look!" He pointed to the lightly falling snow as though it were something he had conjured up especially for her. "It's snowing. Our first snowfall," he murmured, wrapping his arms around her and burying his face in the back of her neck.

His words touched Rita. Was there something in his voice that promised this was only the first of many snowfalls they would share together? Inexplicably, her heart broke rhythm. Somewhere in the back of her mind she had been preparing herself for the day when he would no longer be a part of her life. No, that was wrong, Twigg would always be a part of her life, a most important part. But nothing had been said about their relationship after the coming Christmas when he planned to return to California. It was almost as though she were living each day to its fullest and after that future point in time everything seemed dark and hazy.

His arms tightened around her, his breath warm and soft on her skin. So warm, warmer than the fire's glow which shed the only light into the afternoon's dimness. She felt his desire rising firm and hard against the swell of her buttocks and the insistent caress of his fingers upon the tips of her breasts. He turned her into his embrace, finding her mouth with his own and possessing it with soft and myriad kisses that deepened imperceptibly and aroused her senses to beat in tune with his own.

He drew her down onto the geometric carpet before the hearth; the fire's heat seemed cool and distant in comparison to the warmth he imparted to her flesh as he tenderly stripped away her clothes, leaving them in a heap mingled with his own. His hands caressed her tenderly, tracing the sweet hollows of her body and rounding over the supple, womanly curves of her breasts and belly, wandering in teasing erotic touches to the moist, warm valley where thigh met thigh.

Her clear blue eyes closed then, heightening her perception of his lovemaking. She moved against his fingers and mewed in delight when his lips followed where his hand had explored, tracing her contours with delicate ardor.

Twigg began to tremble with the force of his desire. He reveled in her responses, knowing he had found the woman who could both give and take, who needed this sensuous contact of his flesh upon hers. He wanted to wait, to double her pleasure and watch her rock beneath him with the force of her climax. But the sight of her half-parted lips beckoned to him, tempting him, sounding an echoing note in his very center. Her vulnerability, so much a part of her, deepened his emotions for her while her responsive body appealed for the complete fulfillment she could only share when his flesh entered hers and he claimed her for his own.

His mouth descended upon hers as he parted her thighs and he felt her warm, pulsing flesh welcoming him. Her arms wrapped around his neck, clinging to him, making herself a part of him and he a part of her. He loved to watch her face smile up at him, her mirror blue eyes seeming to fill themselves only with him.

Rita's eyes opened to see him looking down at her, his eyes dark with seduction and passion, the line of his mouth softening and forming the shape of her name. He came to her and took her, this marvelously loving man who had filled her life even more sweetly than he was now filling her body. She did not know if she loved him, did not know if she wanted to love him. Would she ever trust herself to that emotion again? Love demanded so much, it seemed. There were no demands here, only a sharing and a needing and giving. Love had too many sharp edges, able to cut through the soul like a razor, unlike this which seemed to be more a melding and a joining of the heart and the body.

The lines of her body seemed to perfectly match his, meeting him thrust for thrust and driving him closer and closer to the edge of that abyss where he would carry her with him into the shattering void. Her arms held him tightly, her mouth yielded beneath his and she took him into her again and again, deeper, closer, caressing him in undulating waves until he heard the sound of his own pleasure in his ears and she clung to him as they toppled over the edge of carnality into the wondrous garden where soul touched soul.

The world filtered back into consciousness; the flicker of the fire, the soft fall of snow against the window. They had held each other following their simultaneous release, closing their eyes into the shared oblivion, warmed by their pleasure and astounded by the force of their passion.

When she turned, Twigg was looking down at her, watching her through lowered lids. His mossy-green eyes answered all her unasked questions. There was no need to talk about the magic that happened between them.

Sighing, she nestled against his chest and he cradled her close to him, imparting his warmth and stroking her skin. There was so much he wanted to tell her, but he knew she was still skittish as a colt and so very, very vulnerable. There's a place in my life for you, my love, my friend. Could you find a place for me?

*   *   *

Rachel arrived with the first snowfall of the year. Without Rita having to mention it or to ask, Twigg had removed all his personal belongings from her cottage: his razor, his tooth-brush, items of clothing, and notebooks. With each possession he dropped into the paper sack, Rita had become more resentful of her youngest daughter's intrusion.

Looking beautiful in her scarlet parka trimmed in white fur, Rachel was the perfect snow bunny, Rita thought, pushing away her selfish resentment.

Rachel lugged in two sets of skis and poles. "Mom, you wouldn't believe how bad the roads are. If this keeps up through the night, we should have a good surface tomorrow. I came in the back way and they were preparing the ski lift. You have Twigg's number, don't you? I want to make sure he's up for skiing." Rita felt herself flinch but turned and made a pretense of reading the number from the small address book on her desk.

Rita went into the kitchen to make a hot toddy for Rachel. She didn't need to hear the conversation between her daughter and her lover. Didn't want to hear it.

"Thanks, Mummy. I'm going to drink this and hit the sack. Twigg said he was raring to go and would meet me at seven. Don't worry about getting up to see me off. This is one date I won't be late for."

Rita lay in her empty bed aware of a deep loneliness. Twigg should be there with her, just within reach of her hand. She remembered how long it had taken her to become used to sleeping alone once Brett had left. At first, with Twigg, it had taken some doing to get used to sleeping with someone again. Now she was back at square one.

Rolling over, she pounding the pillow. Get used to it now, she told herself. Once Christmas comes and goes, this is the way it's going to be. Lonely.

She ached. She resented. She almost hated. Sleep was fitful and there was no sense in tossing and turning and bemoaning the loss of her lover because Rachel had arrived. Rachel was innocent, and why shouldn't the girl expect to spend some time with her own mother? Rationalizing didn't help. Better to get up for some hot tea and read until she felt drowsy.

Rita scanned her shelves for the new titles Ian had brought, looking for the new Patricia Matthews novel. By page 2 she was hoping to immerse herself in the story. She admired the author's style and her remarkable ability to capture a character's essence.

Rita turned the page, then realized she hadn't the faintest idea what was happening. Rita's mind, seething with frustration and jealousy was simply incapable of concentration. Her big plan, her wonderful surprise, was dashed. The two snowmobiles in the garage were meant to surprise Twigg. She had purchased them weeks ago with the intention of barreling up to Twigg's cottage and inviting him for a ride. Her plan was to skim the snowy mountains for hours, letting the wind whip their cheeks and then come home for hot soup and fresh bread in front of the roaring fireplace. They would make love and lie in each other's arms. They would talk about everything and nothing, have long, comfortable silences, and then make love again, until the fire died and they crept into bed to lie spoon fashion against one another.

Laying her book aside, Rita pulled the belt tighter

about her now slim waist and walked into the cold garage. She stared down at the two shiny machines. All gassed and ready to go. The keys hung on a nail by the garage door, still shiny and unused. She hardly felt the cold as she walked over to peer down at the padded seat with its safety strap. It would have been a wonderful memory.

The snowmobiles would make a smashing present for Charles and Nancy Ames when they arrived after Thanksgiving. If anyone was going to have a wonderful memory, she was glad it was Charles.

Back in the warm living room, Rita shivered. She added another pine log to the fire and sat down on a mound of pillows. She sipped at her lukewarm tea. She couldn't let Rachel's visit throw her into a tizzy. She had to do something, get her act together, as her daughter put it. Wasn't Rachel the one who always said "Go for it"? Did she really want to put up a fight for Twigg? She hated the term "fight for him." If whatever they had between them wasn't stable enough to withstand Rachel's arrival, then she didn't want any part of it.

Eventually, she dozed and woke early when Rachel tiptoed through the living room. "Sorry, Mom, I didn't know if I should wake you or cover you with a blanket. You're going to be stiff and sore from sleeping in that position. Couldn't sleep, huh?"

"I haven't been here all that long, an hour or so," Rita lied. "Can I make you some coffee or something to eat?"

"I already plugged the pot in. I have to meet Twigg in fifteen minutes. How do you like this new ski suit? I just had it made. I wanted to impress the great Tahoe skier. I designed the material myself. What do you think?"

Rita eyed the sky-blue pattern and nodded. "It's beautiful," she said honestly.

Rachel gulped at the scalding coffee. She handed it to her mother. "You'll see me when you see me. Have a nice day, Mom." She was gone.

Rita sighed and headed for the bathroom. She was about to step into the shower when she heard squeals and laughter outside. She parted the curtains in the bathroom and looked out. Twigg was pummeling Rachel with snowballs, to her daughter's delight. Rachel ducked and grabbed Twigg below the knees. Both bundled figures toppled into the snow. Laughing and shouting, they got up and trudged toward the ski lift.

The driving, needle sharp spray did nothing for Rita's mood nor did the brisk toweling. The scented bath powder annoyed her as did the fragrant lotion she applied to her entire body. She dressed and made herself a huge breakfast which she threw away. She was settling down with the Patricia Matthews book when the phone pealed to life.

"Rita? This is Connie Baker. My kids told me they thought they saw you in town the other day. If you aren't doing anything, why don't you come over for lunch and we can spend some time together. I can have Dick pick you up in the Land Rover. What do you say?"

"I'd love to come over. Don't bother sending Dick. I can use the snowmobile. I can leave now if it isn't too early."

"Are you kidding. Yours is the first human voice I've heard except for these kids since I got here. If you have any good books, I'd appreciate a few."

Should she leave a note or not? She sat down at the typewriter and pecked out a brief note:

Rachel,
Took the snowmobile and went visiting.
I don't know when I'll be back.

She signed the brief note and propped it up on the kitchen table between the salt and pepper shakers.

She liked Connie Baker with her down-home approach to life. She was a spunky farm girl from Iowa who, according to her, married a city slicker with more money than brains. She hadn't seen Connie since the divorce, so there would be a lot of catching up to do. A lot of telling on Rita's part. Maybe it was time for her to talk, to confide in someone, and who better than Connie?

Rita felt twelve years old as she skimmed over the hills and fields that led to the Baker property. She brought the whizzing snowmobile to a smooth stop in back of the sprawling ranch-style house and beeped the horn that sounded like a frog. She had forgotten how much fun it was to ride on a snowmobile. She wondered what Brett was going to do with the machine he took from the garage when he moved out the contents. Maybe add a sidecar for Melissa so they could ride down Fifth Avenue on a snowy Sunday morning. She giggled at the thought and then laughed out loud.

There were kisses, hugs, fond looks, and tight grips on each other's shoulders as the two women stared at one another.

"Should we lie to each other now or later how

147

neither of us has changed and we didn't get older, just better?" Connie grinned.

"Why don't we pass on that part and get down to serious talking." Rita laughed. "Tell me, what are you doing with yourself?"

"You know that big ox I married, the one who had more money than brains? He decided life was passing him by and he wanted to taste some of that young stuff out there. We divorced last year, and I'm happy to say that I took everything. Now, I understand his ladylove has taken a job in a drugstore to help pay the rent." Connie laughed, but it was a brittle sound and totally without mirth. "Don't feel sorry for me, Rita, I'm doing the best I can to be as happy as I can. Ask the kids!"

Why should I ask anyone? Rita wondered why Connie thought she wouldn't be believed.

"Hell, being forty-six going on forty-seven is like being born again. Second time around, that kind of thing. Enough of me, tell me about yourself."

Rita sat down with a cup of coffee, propped her stockinged feet on a maple table, and proceeded to fill in her friend on her life during the past year. "I don't know how to handle it, Connie. Rachel is my daughter. How do I deal with that?"

"Just like she was any other woman. She's no kid, Rita. She knows exactly what she's doing. So, you're really caught up in this fella, are you? Tell me what this Twigg Peterson is like."

"He's terrific. Warm, sensitive, loving . . . all the good things I like in a man." Connie heard her friend's voice become soft and shy. Like a young girl's, she thought. "You would like him, Connie. Everyone seems to like Twigg," she said proudly. "I watch him with his friends, my friends. They respond to his sincerity and his concern. He treats people with respect. In some of those unconcerned and impersonal New York restaurants, I've seen waiters respond to his smile and courtesy. No small feat, I can tell you. There's genuine caring between his friends and himself. I saw this one night when he had the Donaldson's stay overnight at his cottage. He has a knack for making everyone feel special. . . ." Rita broke off in midsentence, running her fingers through her shining chestnut hair. "I'm running on like a schoolgirl."

"And you almost look like one," Connie said, eyeing her friend's slimmer waistline and pink, glowing skin. "God, if this guy of yours could bottle that magical rejuvenation he's given you, he'd be a millionaire."

"God, Connie, is that all you think about? Money?"

"It keeps a girl warm at night. Sure, what's wrong with thinking about money?" She said it lazily, offhandedly, but she watched Rita closely. If for one moment this Peterson man was thinking he had found himself a meal ticket, Connie personally would go down to the lake and kill him. When all was said and done, when all the looks were gone, what else was there besides a woman's children and financial security. She would never say this aloud to Rita. Being too much of a romantic, Rita never considered the practical side of life. How else had Brett managed to walk away with so much? Deciding she should steer the conversation along other lines, Connie asked, "Are you thinking of marriage?"

"It's never come up. . . ."

"I didn't ask if this Peterson proposed to you. I didn't even ask if it was something the two of you talked about. I asked if you were thinking about it."

"No . . . that is . . . I just don't know. I only know I don't want to be hurt again."

"Do you expect to be hurt?"

Rita looked at her friend, a claw of anger nicking at the back of her brain. "What kind of question is that?" she demanded.

"Hey, don't go getting your back up. I merely asked if you *expected* to be hurt."

Rita jumped to her feet, pulling her sweater down over her hips. It was a habit acquired from the time when the bulge around the middle needed hiding. "Dammit, Connie! I'm hurting right now!"

"How does this Peterson guy feel about you?" Connie pressed, disregarding Rita's obvious pain. If it was going to be painful, better it be here and now when there was someone to comfort her. Connie was too familiar with lonely, empty bedrooms where there was no one to hear the tears or hold back the loneliness.

Rita pulled a cigarette from Connie's pack and lit it, her hands shaking perceptibly. "I don't know how he feels," she said abruptly, exhaling. "No, that's not true. I *think* he loves me. He acts as though he loves me. Sometimes, when he makes love to me, he calls me his love. But what the hell does that mean, anyway? Men say all kinds of things when they're making love."

"I see. And, of course, you know this from your wide and varied experience, right?"

"Oh, shut up, Connie. No, don't shut up. I need

you to help me." It was a cry, a plea, a dependency on an old friendship.

"Do you love him, Rita?"

"Yes, dammit. As much as I'll allow myself." It was the first time the question had been put to her and her own answer stunned her.

"But?" Connie asked quietly.

"But. Yes, there's always a but, isn't there? It's the age difference. I saw Twigg and Rachel having a snowball fight this morning. They both looked so young, so carefree. So young. My God, Connie, he's only a few years older than Camilla!"

"By my calculations, he's nearly ten years older than Camilla. Quit being a martyr to your age, Rita. It snatches the hope away from the rest of us who've had their fortieth birthdays. And why do you consider the ten years between Twigg and Camilla so negligible and yet the ten years between Twigg and yourself seem so monumental? What's so earth shattering about a little difference in age?" Connie demanded.

Rita plopped down again on the sofa beside her friend. "Okay, you've got something to say. Say it."

"Look at Brett with his twenty-two-year-old wife and look at my ex with his younger-than-springtime girl. In a way, I do admire them. They went for it, as the saying goes. They didn't let me or you or their kids stand in their way. My ex is living on the poverty level with his drugstore queen, but they're happy, damn them. They're happy. Jake came over to see the kids one day, and he confessed that his lover has made him feel like a man, that she didn't care if he was rich or poor. That as long as they would be together they could live anywhere. And he bought it. This is coming from a guy who slept on silk sheets and drove a 450SL Mercedes, who didn't bat an eye at spending a fortune for a vacation. It was hard at first, but I discovered I can live without him and with his money and enjoy it. I wouldn't take him back for anything in the world. I like myself now, who I've become. There's a whole world out there, Rita, a world we never knew about. I can see a difference in you too. You look like you're a person instead of someone's mother or someone's wife. Don't get me wrong, I'm not knocking marriage or mother-hood. I think marriage should be like a driver's license, renewable every few years, before it gets to the point we were at a couple of years ago."

"Have you really become so jaded? What about commitment to one another. What about love?"

"What about it? Commitment, I mean. If having a commitment means suffering, I don't need it and neither do you." Rita felt herself come under Connie's frank stare. "Wasn't that essentially what you were saying before? That you expect to be hurt?"

"No ... yes ... Christ, I don't know! I only know how I feel when I'm with him. How I feel when I'm in his arms."

Connie reached over to pat Rita's hand. "Then enjoy it, friend. Enjoy every minute of it and quit trying to play the odds. Be truthful and honest with yourself and him. Don't pretend to be some-thing you're not. If you win, you'll have the satis-faction of knowing you've done it on the fair and square. If you lose, you'll have nothing to regret, wondering if you should have done this or said that. Games are for children, Rita, and they play by childish rules."

They sat for hours talking about their lives, their dreams and expectations. They discussed mutual friends, Rita's career, their grandchildren, and Connie's man-friend who had a lot of brains and absolutely no money. "He's a tree surgeon." She laughed delightedly. "And I want to tell you he's one hell of a hunk in bed. I get orgasmic just thinking about him. He actually listens to me when I talk. He respects my opinions and he thinks I'm as poor as he is. He thinks this place is my uncle's and the big house in Scarsdale belongs to my parents. I know my money would scare him off. He's a fine man, Rita, and I love him. You want to hear something crazy, something really off the wall?" Rita nodded. "I'm toying with giving my ex his money back and getting myself an apartment someplace and starting all over. The kids are all in college now or married. They're leading their own lives so I should be leading mine. I have a good job with the same advertising agency, and there's talk of making me a partner. With a lot of hard work I can make it. Joe thinks I can, anyway. If you know anyone who needs trees cut, let me know. He's fully insured so there's no problem."

Rita stared at Connie and then doubled over laughing. She laughed till the tears flowed. Connie joined in and then they were both rolling on the floor, laughing and crying hysterically.

"And those smart-ass kids of ours think we don't know where we're coming from," Connie gasped, wiping at her eyes.

"Or where we're going," Rita said through peals

of laughter. "What time is it? I should be getting back."

"Why?"

Rita laughed again. "Beats me. It seemed like the thing to say. We've covered about all of it."

"How about a hot buttered rum before you start out? You'll freeze your tushy off if you go out there without being fortified."

"You got it. Don't spare the rum."

Rita looked at her watch. Her eyes widened in shock. It was three-ten. Where had the time gone? Who cared; she'd had the time of her life and didn't regret one minute of the time she'd spent with her old friend.

It was two minutes after four on her digital watch when she drove the snowmobile into the garage. She was climbing out of the seat when the door opened. Twigg stood outlined in the doorway, Rachel beside him.

"Mom, where in the hell have you been?"

"Didn't you get my note?"

"Of course I got your note, but you didn't say where you were going!" Rachel said accusingly.

"You keep reminding me of my age, Rachel, and at my age I don't think I have to check in or out with you unless you want to show me the same courtesy."

Twigg and Rachel stood aside, but not before Rita saw the look of relief in his eyes. He cared.

"You smell like a distillery," Rachel snapped.

"Really. I suppose hot buttered rum will do that," Rita said by way of explanation.

"Where did you get those snowmobiles? I thought Dad took ours."

"I bought them. They belong to me. Any other questions, Rachel?"

"I was worried about you. I didn't even know we had snowmobiles."

Twigg's voice was soft, concerned, but not accusing. "Glad you got back in one piece. This child here wouldn't let me leave till you got back. I tried to tell her you were okay, but she wasn't buying."

Rita's eyes thanked him. She wondered if he had kissed Rachel. Or if Rachel had kissed him. It wasn't important. "Thanks for staying with Rachel."

"Any time. I've never been on a snowmobile. Would you mind taking me for a spin tomorrow and showing me the ropes?"

"Love to. What time?" Rita called over her shoulder as she made her way to the bathroom.

"Noonish, if that's okay with you. I have a little research I want to do in the morning."

"Sounds good to me," Rita called back as she closed the bathroom door.

Rachel's voice carried clearly and distinctly. "Hey, what about me?" she wanted to know.

"No sidecars. Guess you'll have to ski. Rita doesn't ski," Twigg said casually.

The silence was thunderous with the closing of the door. Rita switched the bathroom fan on and stripped down. The hot, steamy shower left her squeaky clean. She felt satisfied, even smug. She had really carried it off!

Chapter Nine

$\mathcal{A}$ STATE OF UNDECLARED COLD WAR EXISTED IN the Bellamy cottage over the next few days. Rachel was in turns sullen and then ecstatic when Twigg spent time with her. Her eyes would fall sharply on her mother when she went out with Twigg to the ski slopes or the resort lodge for a few drinks and dancing. There was a gleam of triumph in Rachel's eyes when Twigg would ask Rita to come with them and she would automatically refuse. "Isn't he polite?" Rachel said on more than one occasion, and Twigg's eyes would fall on Rita with dark questions in their depths.

At these times of Rachel's brutal tactlessness, Twigg would watch Rita's face pale and see a shard of pain pierce her eyes. He would feel the impulse to take her in his arms, to kiss away the hurt. He could easily find excuses not to spend time alone with Rachel, but was that really Rita's answer? He didn't believe it was. Rita had to learn to trust him and to believe in herself as an attractive, desirable woman. If she saw younger women as her competition, she must learn to deal with it even if one of those young women was her daughter. To ignore Rachel or to pretend to dislike or be bored by her would be a lie and unfair. He could only hope that the next time he invited Rita to join them she would accept his invitation.

Rita's pain was sharp and acute and there was nothing to do for it. She took to insulating herself by cooking and cleaning and going to town with the laundry. Rachel knows, Rita guessed intuitively. She knows I've been sleeping with Twigg and she knows I care for him. And yet, it doesn't deter her from flirting with him, almost seducing him right under my nose. Don't do this to me, Rachel, she thought. Don't force me to a choice, because right now, I don't think I like you very much. Your "go for it" attitude should not include "going" for Twigg. Especially if you suspect he's become my lover and is very special to me.

The fault was not Twigg's. Rachel usually got what she went after. The captaincy of the cheerleaders, the big man on campus, the right job, the right friends. Once Rachel set her sights, there was no stopping her. How could Twigg be blamed? Rachel was young, vital, and exciting. And so very, very determined.

On Thanksgiving Day Rita was peeling carrots for dinner by the kitchen sink when she lifted her head and looked out the window. At the end of the property was a small gully. When the children were little they used to ride their sleds down the hill and then squeal with delight when they toppled into the gully. Rachel, cherry-red parka brilliant against the snow, was sledding down the hill, knowing full well she would topple over. Twigg was still on top of the hill, head thrown back, laughing.

As predicted, Rachel toppled, Twigg fast behind her. It was inevitable that he would lift her to her feet and that his lips would find hers. Or was it Rachel who leaned into Twigg's embrace? She stared a moment longer, her eyes misted, and she quickly moved away from the window. She didn't see Twigg push Rachel away, nor did she see him lift his eyes in the direction of the kitchen window. She wasn't sure what she felt, was uncertain as to what she should do. When in doubt, do nothing, she told herself. That's nothing, as in zero. Zilch.

"Why did you do that?" Twigg asked Rachel, anger ripping his voice.

"Do what?" Rachel feigned innocence.

"You know. Why did you kiss me like that? I like to decide who and when I'm going to kiss someone."

"For God's sake. You almost sound like my mother," Rachel pouted.

"Your mother happens to be a wonderful woman and a beautiful person and I value her friendship. In short, Rachel, I happen to like your mother, a lot more than I like you!"

Rachel was shocked; no one had ever said they preferred someone else to her. Much less her own mother! Not even her father, who adored his youngest daughter. "Have you been sleeping with my mother?" Rachel demanded. "You have, haven't you! I thought so! It's written all over her. Dear old Mummy. I can't believe it! God, you aren't much older than I am. What would you want with her?"

Twigg seized Rachel's arm, shaking her furiously, his face set and murderous. "Don't you talk about her that way. Why don't you open your eyes and see her for the lovely woman she is rather than just seeing her as your mother? She's been a friend to you, Rachel, and you've betrayed her, and I hope to God she never knows. What your mother and I mean to one another is no concern of yours. Is that clear?"

"Very clear," Rachel hissed, the fury of rejection beating wild within her. Was it true what he said? That her mother was lovely and wonderful? How could it be? Rita was already in her forties! She was old! *She was her mother!*

"Why can't you see her for the person she is, Rachel? Oh, I know you think you're a grown woman, but you are also a selfish child. Perhaps you are woman enough to give of yourself to someone you love deeply. But all of us remain children, selfish children, where our parents are concerned, making demands for complete love and total attention, forgetting that our parents are people first and parents second. Think about it, Rachel."

Rachel was humiliated. She didn't need this man to tell her how to feel about her parents, much less how to feel about her own mother! "Very well, O lord and master, I will think about it!" she snapped, bowing from the waist in mock respect. "But before I do, tell me. Has my mother been properly grateful for the attentions of a young stud like you?"

At the rage suffusing his face, Rachel stepped

backwards. She hung her head in shame for her coarse remark. She liked Twigg and she loved her mother. It was only that she had never been rejected this way before, especially not in favor of her mother. Mothers were supposed to be self-sacrificing and interested only in their children's happiness. They weren't supposed to reach out and take that happiness for themselves.

"What you need, Rachel," Twigg was saying, looming over her, "is a good swift kick in the ass. A pity someone hasn't done it before now."

"C'mon," Rachel cajoled, "we were having such fun. Why spoil it? So okay, I'm sorry I got you in a clinch. I'll even tell old Mummy it was me who trapped you. She saw us, you know. She was standing by the kitchen sink. Probably spying."

"She wasn't spying. Rita would never lower herself. That's something you would do, isn't it, Rachel?" His tone revealed his total disgust.

"If it was important to me, yes, I would!"

"What about trust and faith?"

"You've gotta be kidding. The man hasn't been born a woman can trust and believe. Look what my father did to her. Even my own father! And you call me a child, Twigg Peterson. You have some growing up to do yourself."

Twigg clenched his fists. He wanted to push her down into the snow and rub her face in it till she screamed for mercy. "If men are like that, Rachel, it's because of women like you. One more thing, if you so much as say one word about this incident to Rita, I swear you'll have to deal with me. Make certain you understand, Rachel. I mean it. I won't have Rita hurt."

Rachel stared into his challenging green eyes.

161

What she saw frightened her. "Okay, staunch defender of middle-aged women. Now that you've spoiled the day, I think I'll go back to the house and read a book. A good book! None of that unrealistic crap my mother writes."

"Why are your mother's books so unrealistic, Rachel? Because she writes about relationships? Real people and their emotions and their love? Yes, I can see where that would seem unreal to you."

Twigg flopped down onto the Magic Flyer and wrapped his arms around his snow-covered knees. He stared at the kitchen window for a long time, willing Rita to materialize. He felt there was a large hole in his stomach that was gradually sucking up his chest. Whatever he felt for Rita Bellamy was stronger than any emotion he had ever felt for another woman. She was warmth. She was comfort. She was intelligent and loving; she was Rita Bellamy. His love. A part of himself that could not be denied. They had searched for, found, and touched each other. Was that love? He grinned. Yes, he was in love, did love. This special, fragile woman whom he yearned to protect and yet realized he admired. He wanted her to fulfill herself as a woman, as a person. He wanted her to remain in charge of her own life; he only wanted to share it with her. There was no way around it. He wanted to love her.

It was a small word, according to Rita. It didn't take much space on a page, yet it was awesome. It was a word capable of changing two lives, shaping the destiny of both.

Twigg dusted off his pants and then picked up the sled. He tramped up the hill toward the Bellamy cottage. He wasn't sorry for the way he had spoken to Rachel. It was time someone set her straight. He leaned the sled against the side of the garage. He opened the kitchen door and shouted. "I'll see you later, Rita."

"Okay," she called back from somewhere deep in the cottage. A sigh of relief escaped him. She sounded fine. Trust and faith. She trusted him, believed in him regardless of what she had seen through the window. That was what it was all about.

While the turkey basted itself, Rita curled herself into the deep love seat by the fire and started to read. She was surprised, after an hour or so, that she was really comprehending what she was reading. She wasn't engulfed in the scene she had witnessed.

Rachel walked into the room carrying two cups of coffee. "When are we eating? I'm starved!" she complained.

"Then eat something. We're not going to eat till around seven. That's the time I told Twigg to come over."

"Why did you invite him anyway?" Rachel snapped.

"I invited him because I wanted to invite him. The two of us certainly cannot eat a thirteen-pound turkey. Thanksgiving is for sharing or have you forgotten?"

"It depends on what you're sharing?" Rachel snapped.

"Is that supposed to mean something in particular?" Rita asked evenly.

"It means whatever you want it to mean," Rachel almost snarled.

Rita felt the most uncontrollable urge to slap her daughter and send her to her room. "Rachel, don't talk in riddles. If you have something to say, I suggest you say it and get it over with," Rita said levelly, her gaze keen and direct.

Rachel dropped her eyes. "For two cents, I'd leave and go back to the city, but the road to the highway is closed."

Rita made a mental note to call Connie and ask her to have her son plow her out to the main road. Nothing must keep her from Charles's game the next day.

"Why don't you take a nap till dinner is ready. I'll call you so you can mash the turnips."

"Call me after they're mashed. Let your friend Twigg do it, after all he's freeloading, isn't he?"

"No, he isn't freeloading. I invited him. However, if you want to get into technicalities, I don't recall inviting you. You called and announced that you were coming. Either keep a civil tongue in your mouth or don't speak. I mean it, Rachel. I've had enough of your sly innuendos. If you want to say something, now is the time to say it. If not, stay off my space."

Rachel stared at her mother, stunned at her words. She turned and fled as though a dog was snapping at her heels.

Exhausted, Rita fell back onto the couch. Damn, she hated confrontations. Especially with Rachel.

Twigg arrived early, eager to help with the last-minute preparations for dinner. He worked beside her in the small kitchen, sipping his wine and making small talk. Lord, how she enjoyed being with this man. She glanced up, seeing the window through which she had seen Rachel and Twigg kissing. It was dark now, mirroring Twigg and herself working happily side by side. Strange how the same window could look out to a hurt and look inward to a pleasure. Twigg followed Rita's gaze, meeting hers in the dark glass. As if knowing what she was thinking, he wrapped his arms around her, pressing his lips against her hair. "They look happy, don't they, that couple in the window. How lucky we are to be inside looking out."

She leaned back against him, feeling his warmth and recognizing the sweet, fruity aroma of the wine on his breath. Is that what we are, she asked herself, a couple? Is that how he thinks of himself and me? She looked again, seeing them reflected there. He was tall, leaning over her, holding her. She fit into the circle of his arms so naturally, so willingly.

"It's Thanksgiving, love," he murmured against the side of her neck, "and we have many blessings to be grateful for." His embrace held her fast and his lips found hers.

Yes, she thought, sighing, leaning against him, catching sight of the window again, there are many blessings, and the most precious one is you.

Dinner was delicious and enjoyable. Rita and Twigg talked animatedly, their eyes meeting and lingering. Rachel picked at her food, her mind otherwise occupied. From time to time Rita looked at her daughter and forced her into polite conversation.

Whatever had happened between Twigg and Rachel out there in the backyard, Twigg seemed to have handled it. Rachel was subdued and thoughtful but not hostile. At least not hostile or angry toward Twigg, Rita thought disdainfully. I'm another matter entirely. Somehow, I've disappointed her and I'm not certain how. She wondered, not for the first time, does Rachel guess that Twigg and I are lovers? Is that the source of the disappointment? That my morals are somehow lacking, unworthy of a mother? How easily these young people decide what's right for them and at the same time deplore and condemn the same values in their parents. It doesn't matter. Not really. Rachel, being Rachel, will soon come to terms with it. While the girl has never displayed prolonged loyalty or interest in any one person or thing, she also doesn't harbor ill feelings and anger. Whatever, it's Rachel's problem and she'll have to deal with it.

The conversation drifted around to the football game the following afternoon. "Why don't you go with Mother?" Rachel asked Twigg snidely. "I'm certain she'd love taking you with her and introducing you to all the family."

Twigg's eyes met Rita's. "In the first place, I have not been invited. Secondly, I have work to do." Silently, he told Rita that he realized it would complicate things if he were to go with her. She needed this time with Charles and her own feelings.

Wordlessly, Rita thanked him.

"How about a game of chess, Twigg?" Rachel asked as he took his pie plate to the sink.

"Later. I want to help Rita with the dishes. I know those three-inch nails of yours don't get themselves into dishwater," he teased.

Not for the first time Rita was aware that he

usually referred to her by her name instead of saying, "I want to help your mother with the dishes." She was Rita Bellamy, to Twigg. Not Rachel's mother. How nice, just to be herself.

Later, Twigg played chess with Rachel while Rita busied herself with her needlepoint. She would feel his eyes fall on her, and when she lifted her head she could read the message they spoke.

When Rita awoke the next morning she looked outside. Connie had been as good as her word. Her oldest son, Dick, had arrived sometime during the wee hours and plowed the road.

Rachel could go back to the city now, if she chose. Yet Rita knew her daughter would still be in the cottage when she returned. Perhaps she herself would spend the night in a motel rather than make the long trip back on the same day.

Twigg was waiting for her when she drove the car around the bend. Rita rolled down the window. "What are you doing up so early?" she asked, laughing at his rumpled hair and the stubble of beard on his chin.

"I couldn't let you go off without telling you to drive carefully and to hurry back. You're very special to me, lady, I hope you know that."

Interstate 80 was free of snow, and Rita felt her shoulder muscles relax. It would be a good trip. She switched on the radio and heard Kenny Rogers singing "Lady." She grinned, remembering Twigg's departing words. She was glad he had kept it light between them. She didn't want any declarations of love and promises that couldn't be kept. Being "special" could mean so many things. It didn't necessarily mean love.

"Do you expect to be hurt?" Connie had asked her. Rita pulled her thoughts away from Twigg. She should be thinking about Brett and what she would say when she saw him. It had been a long time. Because of the tickets Charles had sent them, they would be sitting next to one another all through the game. Somehow, she would face it when the time came. She wouldn't worry about it now. Instead, she concentrated on Kenny Rogers and wished he would sing the song again.

Stopping at a restaurant for lunch, Rita delayed and lingered over coffee so she would arrive at the stadium just before game time. There was no point in arriving early and bearing up under the strain of spending all her time with Brett and his new wife.

Walking outside into the chill after the warmth of the restaurant, she was glad she had worn her mink jacket and high, fleece-lined boots. She wished Twigg was with her so the two of them could cheer for Charles. Twigg would like her son, and Charles would like Twigg. Perhaps, at first, there would be some resentment, but later they would learn to appreciate one another. She laughed uneasily. Whatever gave her the idea there would ever be a "later"? Now, and only now, was all that was important.

It was like old home week when Rita took her seat in the crowded college stadium. Surprisingly, Camilla and Tom were there. Brett hadn't yet made his appearance. Camilla wrapped her arms around her mother. "Tom said we had to come and root for Charles. We had a devil of a time getting tickets though. We're two rows ahead of you."

"I'm so glad you came, honey. Charles will be so happy to have all of us here. He has a girl," Rita whispered. "He's bringing her up to the cottage next weekend."

"We had our dinner with Tom's folks. I'm glad I came, Mom. Family is, and should be, very important." Rita steeled herself for Camilla's diatribe on family closeness, complete with charged and veiled statements concerning one's duty to family solidarity. Instead, she heard her oldest daughter say, "The kids miss you, Mom. Let's not be angry with one another. Maybe one of these days I'll understand and I'll handle it better. Just hang in there with me, okay?"

"Okay," Rita said softly, hardly daring to believe her ears. "You'd better take your seat. I'll see you later. They're tuning up for the 'National Anthem.' "

Tom put his arm around Camilla and looked at her approvingly. He leaned over from his tall, rangy height to plant a kiss on Rita's cheek. "Do you know how wonderful you look?" he asked.

She laughed; the sound was carefree and almost girlish to her own ears. "I feel wonderful, Tom."

"Daddy isn't here?" Camilla complained.

"He will be, don't worry. He probably had trouble getting a parking space. Are you warm enough? I brought a blanket."

"We did too. Keep it, it must be all of ten degrees."

There were three minutes to play in the first quarter when Brett arrived with his wife. Rita's eyes widened in surprise as he ushered Melissa past pairs of knees. "Rita," he said pleasantly, "this is Melissa."

"Hello." Rita smiled at the young, dark-haired

woman. How young, was her first thought. How pretty and wholesome, was her second. How very, very pregnant, was her third! It was a shock, but not unpleasant. Funny, Camilla had never mentioned Melissa's pregnancy. Did she think her mother would be devastated by the news? Truthfully, Rita knew that only months ago it would have sent her into a panic and a depression. Now, since Twigg, she had gained a different perspective.

Brett looked happy. Happier than she had seen him in years. Contented. A contentment and excitement that she had once been responsible for, when she was young and hugely pregnant. And Brett looks younger too, she thought, softer and somehow more mellow. He's not fighting for his identity; his ego is intact. How awful it must have been for him when he was so insecure and uncertain of his place as her husband, of his masculinity and position as head of the household. Her career and its rewards had stripped him of that, she knew. Money was freedom and, according to Brett, possessed a masculine gender. Freedom was for men, just like power. She was glad to see he wasn't shattered by the changes she had wrought in his life. He had been and still was very important to both her and their children.

Melissa glanced up at Brett when he tucked a thick blanket around her knees. She adores him, Rita saw. Did I look up at him that way? Of course I did, when all I wanted from him was love and security. As soon as I wanted more, like support and understanding and respect, that's when he began to balk. Men like Brett revered women, they didn't respect them—there was a difference.

Like gallant, white knights their image of themselves only shines through a woman's adoring eyes.

A sudden thought stunned Rita. Brett hadn't deserted her after all! He hadn't divorced her because he had found her lacking. No, to the contrary, he had found Rita, the young, adoring, dependent Rita all over again in Melissa! His new wife was probably the same person Rita had been at the same tender age!

Pleased with her realization, Rita sat back and watched the playing field. How nice to know that Brett had loved the life he had shared with her enough that he had actively sought to duplicate it. She had not been so much a failure as a wife and mother if he sought the same things in Melissa. Brett was positively beaming, proud as a rooster and just a little pathetic. What would happen, Rita wondered, if Melissa proved to be a "late bloomer" as she was?

"Are Camilla and Tom here?" Brett asked. "Where's Rachel?"

"Camilla and Tom are two rows ahead of us. Rachel is still up at the lake. She wants to do some skiing." She saw Brett's eyes go to his wife and her chattering teeth. Poor thing, her coat barely covered her stomach. She must be freezing. Rita removed the heavy plaid robe from her knees and nudged Brett. "Here. Give this to Melissa. She's cold."

Brett rewarded her with a smile. How well she remembered those smiles. They used to light up her life during those early years. When had smiles ceased to be enough?

Melissa seemed a bit wary of taking her husband's ex-wife's blanket. "I'll just go down and squeeze in between Camilla and Tom," Rita said. "It was nice to see you, Brett. Very nice. Melissa, much happiness with your new baby." The young girl nodded and tried to smile, pulling the blanket closer around her. "Brett, why don't you take Melissa home? This is no time for her to get sick. I'll explain to Charles. He'll understand."

"If you think he'll understand, okay," Brett said, relieved.

"Before you go, can you spare a minute for Camilla and Tom? They'd like to say 'hello.' "

Brett looked at Rita, thinking how wonderful she looked. Fresher, more confident ... something he couldn't put a finger on. There was a style about her, a certain flair ... a man. It was a man! The thought saddened him. Rita had so much to offer a man, this he knew from experience. Warmth, tenderness, loyalty. Why hadn't she been able to offer him those things when they were married? Why had she insisted on pursuing that silly career? Melissa was holding on to his arm to keep her balance. No matter, Brett thought with certainty. He had Melissa now, and this time he was going to be certain *this* wife didn't get crazy ideas!

Camilla was stunned when she looked up at her father and stepmother. Her father hadn't said a word about the baby. Clearly, talking on the phone every day and seeing were two different things.

Melissa and Camilla hugged and Brett and Tom shook hands. It was obvious to Rita that they all shared warm feelings for one another and she realized she was glad. Brett had divorced her, not the children, and it would be unfair to expect them to take sides against their father. Brett lovingly assisted Melissa up the stairs to the exit, a protective arm about her. Camilla approached Rita excitedly. "My God, Mother, my kids will be that baby's nieces and nephews. Tom, say something!" Her husband grinned at Rita and went back to watching the game.

"Mother say something."

Rita laughed. "Camilla, your father is deliriously happy. Let him enjoy it. You may feel uncomfortable for a while, but eventually you'll get used to the idea. Now watch your brother; he has the ball."

After the game in the Knife and Fork, the campus coffee shop, Rita waited along with Camilla and Tom for Charles and his girl, Nancy.

"I wonder what she's like," Camilla speculated.

"I'm kind of curious myself." Rita smiled.

"If I know Charles, she's probably centerfold material. He always goes for the flash." Tom grinned.

Charles walked in, his hair damp and slicked back. A young girl in a heavy jacket with a hood was beside him. How big he looked. How tiny she looked. There was an air of protectiveness about Charles when he gently pushed the girl forward. "Mom, Camilla, Tom, this is Nancy Ames. Nancy, this is my family. Where's Dad?"

Rita quickly explained. She dreaded the look on her son's face. Instead, she saw it split in an ear-to-ear grin. "You're kidding! That's great. Maybe it'll be a boy and I can take him under my wing."

Nancy slid into the booth. "I've read all your books, Mrs. Bellamy. I think they're super. All the girls in the dorm read them. We don't pass them around either; we each buy our own."

"That's so nice to hear." Rita smiled. Charles preened. His girl read his mom's books and liked them. Hell, what more could a guy ask for?

Was she mistaken or was there a new note of respect in Camilla's eyes?

"Are we all set for this weekend, Mom?" Charles asked.

"All set. I even went out and bought two snowmobiles. His and hers, so to speak. That snow is going to be around for a long time. I'm glad you're coming up, Charles. I have a friend I want you to meet. His name is Twigg Peterson. I think you're going to like him." The statement bubbled out of her and she realized how good it felt to say those words. Charles and Twigg would like one another, and the thought pleased her. She wanted her children to know the man in her life. Seeing Brett again with her new confidence and this sense of herself had relieved her of the burden of the past. She could be free of old memories and ancient hurts and could look to the future. She could believe in herself and could trust in love. Twigg's love.

"I'd like to spend more time with you, but I have a long drive ahead of me. Camilla, call me next week. Remember, any time you want to come up, the door is open. Tom, take care of her for me. Nancy, it was nice meeting you. When you come up, I'll have a copy of the bound galleys for my new book. Perhaps you'd like to see what a book looks like before it gets to the bookstore."

"Charles, do you need anything?" she whispered in his ear as she hugged him.

"I'm okay, Mom. Dulcie sent the brownies. In fact, she sends a batch regularly now. I'll see you on the weekend. This Twigg guy, is he the one Rachel bent my ear about?"

"One and the same." Rita laughed.

"She struck out, huh?" Charles whispered in her ear. Rita shrugged. "You always were a class act, Mom." He kissed her soundly on both cheeks and then walked her to the door. "Drive carefully. It's supposed to snow again this evening."

"I'll be careful and, Charles, I like your girl."

"I knew you would. See you, Mom."

"See you, son."

Chapter Ten

Rita SWUNG THE CAR ONTO THE INTERSTATE, hoping she could reach the lake before it began snowing again. It had been an enlightening afternoon, and she was glad she had gone to Charles's game. Seeing Brett and Melissa had relieved her of those last vestiges of guilt, and she felt lighter now, as if she had shrugged off a heavy cloak. Oh, she knew it wouldn't always be that simple; one just didn't wipe away over twenty years of marriage. But she was making a good start. The guilt she had carried for not being the wife Brett wanted and the mother her children expected was unfair and unjust. She would have nothing more to do with it. She hadn't traded her family and those she loved for the glory of a career or pursuing her own selfish interests. She was neither wife, nor mother, nor best-selling author. "Those are the things I do," she said aloud as though to reaffirm her decision, "those are things I do and not who I am."

Who am I? The answer came easily. I'm a woman who loves a man. I love Twigg. I'll fight for him if I must, even if my adversary is my own daughter. Twigg understood. She loved him and, more, she trusted him. Even with her innermost and tenderest of feelings.

Perhaps Connie had known what she was asking of Rita. "Do you expect to be hurt?" At the time, Rita had missed the point. The truth was that she did. Always had.

She'd expected to be hurt by her children just because they were all growing as people, no longer babies to be cuddled and burped. That was a rough one, letting go. If the fact escaped her before this, she now faced the truth. She had sold them short, each one of them, Camilla, Rachel, and Charles. She had sent out unspoken but clear signals that cried, Need me! I'm your mother! I'll always be here for you! Only Rachel had struck out on her own, becoming independent. And because Rita feared losing her altogether, she had catered to Rachel, refusing to censor, even silently, the girl's most selfish and promiscuous behavior.

Making loans she never expected to be repaid, buying expensive gifts, becoming an easily available baby-sitter . . . it all amounted to the same thing. She had demanded her children prove their love by remaining dependent upon her. And when she had had enough and withdrew, they naturally resented it. The whole pattern was destructive, both to them and herself. Thank heavens she had seen it before it was too late! She might have destroyed her children, sacrificed them to her own needs. And in the end when they turned on her, and they would have, she would have seen herself as their victim! Just the way her own mother felt victimized when Rita turned away from her.

Victim. It had an ugly, unpleasant sound. Was that what Connie had meant? Did she realize Rita expected to be a victim? Did she expect to be hurt?

Rita had expected to be hurt when she saw Brett again. Instead, the meeting had given her new insights about who she had been and who she was now. Was it her image of herself as a victim that kept her from admitting her love to Twigg? Was that the real barrier and not the difference in their ages?

The snow was falling steadily, thick, heavy flakes freezing to the windshield.

Rita kept her eyes glued to the road. She was a fool to start out in such weather conditions. God, where were the plows, the snow trucks with their ashes and salt? Home, eating leftover turkey, she answered herself. Annoyed with the radio, she switched it off. She didn't need to be reminded that driving conditions were hazardous. If there was anything to be glad about, it was that her car had front-wheel drive.

An hour to drive under normal conditions, two with this weather, possibly even three before she would make the Whitehaven turnoff.

She blessed the tiny red lights in front of her. They were like a beacon for her and helped her stay on the road. God, how her eyes ached. Her shoulders were hunched over as she strained to see through the driving, swirling snow. Fearfully, she noticed the sluggishness of the windshield wipers. Not ice, please God, not ice. If the wipers froze, she was in real trouble.

A low rumble behind her made her look into the rearview mirror. A snowplow. She inched over as far as she dared to let him pass her. Once the ash was spread, she could follow him, providing he was going past Whitehaven. Surely, he was just ashing the interstate and not the turnoffs or side roads.

The wipers were freezing badly now and needed to be scraped. Visibility, however, was better as the glow from the truck's taillights provided her with a small beacon to follow. At least she was staying on the road with the ash for traction.

It had been a long time since she prayed. Far too long. To do so now seemed like cheating. Instead, she blessed herself and said her children's names over and over. For the life of her she couldn't remember the names of her grandchildren. For sure she would never make "Mother of the Year." Mother of the Year would remember her grandchildren's names.

She couldn't see, the red lights in front of her were now barely visible. Her back window was full of snow and the side mirror frozen stiff with ice and sleet. She had to stop and pray that if there were anyone behind her, he would stop in time.

Her fingers were numb in their thin leather casing as she tried to chip and pry at the frozen wipers. Tears gathered in her soft blue eyes and instantly froze on her eyelashes. There was no point in trying the passenger side. She did the best she could and climbed back into the car. The twin red lights were specks in the distance. She accelerated slowly and caught up to the snowplow. Her grip in the sodden leather gloves was fierce, and her shoulders felt as though she was carrying a twenty-pound load.

She drove steadily for what seemed like hours. The huge road signs were covered with snow. God, how was she to know when she reached the Whitehaven turnoff? There was something there, but what was it? A marker, an identifying mark of some kind. If only she could remember. A campground sign, that's what it was. She had to watch for a turnoff with a double sign. She switched on the radio and got nothing but static. She turned it off and felt like crying. How stupid she was. What if she had an accident and died all alone out here on an interstate highway? When would she be found? Who would mourn her? What would Twigg feel? What would he say? If only she knew. Crazy wretched thoughts filled her mind as she continued to follow the ash truck.

She was so intent on planning her own funeral she almost missed the sign. A sob caught in her throat. She maneuvered the car slowly off the road and up the curving ramp. She turned right and saw the lights for the truck stop. Inching her way down the snowy road, she turned into the well-filled lot where the lights gleamed and sparkled like Christmas lights.

The warmth and steam from inside hit her like a blast furnace. She looked for a vacant seat and sat down. A beefy trucker moved his heavy jacket and looked at her sympathetically. "Bad out there, huh?" She nodded and ordered a cup of black coffee from the waitress. The young, friendly girl looked at her, took in the mink coat and designer boots. "Is your name Rita?"

181

"Yes, why?" Lord, she didn't need another fan tonight.

"Some guy's been in here six, maybe seven, times looking for a woman in a mink coat. You match his description. There's somebody out there looking for you, lady. He's like a phantom; he comes and goes on a red snowmobile."

"He's been riding up and down the interstate," the trucker with the heavy jacket volunteered.

"Said for you to wait if you got here before he got back. I wish my boyfriend would worry about me like that," the waitress said, placing the cup in front of Rita.

"Jody, and David, that's their names," Rita said triumphantly.

"Whose names?" the waitress asked, inching away from Rita.

"My grandchildren. What time was the man with the snowmobile last in here?"

"An hour at least, wouldn't you say?" the waitress asked the trucker.

"Yeah, a good hour. He's about due. We got bets on him around here."

"I bet you do. I have a kind of bet myself." Rita smiled.

"He your husband?" the trucker asked curiously.

"No," Rita said quietly.

"Oh, one of those."

"Yeah, one of those." Rita grinned.

"Nothing wrong with that." The trucker grinned back.

"My sentiments exactly," Rita said over the rim of her coffee cup.

The door opened. Rita's head jerked up. Her world stood in the doorway.

"Hi, I heard you were looking for me."

"Didn't have anything to do. Lady, you scared the goddamn living hell out of me," Twigg said sitting down next to her. His eyes never left hers. "You okay?" Rita nodded.

"You look like you're frozen," she said. She couldn't tear her eyes away from his.

"Frozen! I'm too numb to feel it if I am. They got bets running on me here, did you know that?"

"I heard. Drink this coffee," she said, pushing her mug toward him.

"The roads are impassable. I think we can both ride the snowmobile. Tight fit."

"I like tight fits," she said, her eyes still on his.

"So do I." His voice was husky and there were shadowy secrets in his eyes. She took his hands, warming them in hers. Her head fell against his shoulder and she felt his lips brush her hair.

Twigg heard her sigh, felt the treasured weight of her head on his shoulder. She was quiet, so quiet. "Penny for your thoughts, love."

"I was just thinking that maybe it's time we talked about that small word," Rita murmured.

"Are we talking about that small word that's so awesome? You mean 'love'?" The shadows in his eyes lifted and he gazed at her sharply, steadily. There would never be a backing away with this man. His honesty would prevent it.

"That's the one."

"You ready to talk about it?" he questioned.

"I think so." Rita grinned.

"Don't think, Rita, my love. With me, you've got to know for certain."

"I *know* so. Let's go home."

"Your place or mine," he teased, that familiar, seductive glint visible in his eyes.

"Yours. I have a guest."

They laughed with each other, standing to leave the diner, eager to be alone with one another. Impetuously, Twigg took her into his arms, lifting her chin to kiss her softly on the lips. Rita was oblivious to the eyes and stares from the others in the diner; she only knew she was in Twigg's arms, being kissed by him, being wanted by him.

He hurried her out into the cold night. Their night. The snow was falling steadily, silently. Breathless, exhilarated by his nearness, Rita found herself once again in his embrace. She lifted her face for his kiss, unashamed to ask for it now, and she felt his lips trembling against hers.

He held her in the circle of his arms; she felt him strong and tall against her. This was her love. He had waited for her to learn about herself. He had trusted her to do so. She now knew she didn't need to be a perfect, stereotypical mother. She did not need to feel guilty for wanting to be more than a wife and homemaker. What she did need, Twigg offered: to be a woman with him, the lover who touched her soul and knew her for the woman she was and not for the roles all women must play.

I love him, for all I am and for all I can be.

Return to the *Captive* novels from
the incomparable

FERN
MICHAELS

*Blazing, passionate novels,
exotic settings, unforgettable love!*

CAPTIVE PASSIONS
CAPTIVE EMBRACES
CAPTIVE SPLENDORS
CAPTIVE INNOCENCE
CAPTIVE SECRETS

Look for the novels of

FERN MICHAELS

in your local bookstore.
Published by Ballantine Books.